"Could we start agai

He lowered his head, his lips almost touching hers. Then he was kissing her again. This time she felt his hunger and it drew her to him. His tongue moistened her lips before plunging deep inside the cavern of her mouth. She felt his hand at the back of her head, holding her to him as he continued to blow her mind. She heard him groan, then he was backing away, making the heat of the day drop to below freezing.

She wanted his arms around her. She wanted him to kiss her some more, make love to her. She was putty in his arms, encircled by the scent and strength and touch of him. But he was Cole Masters. *The* Cole Masters. Playboy of the western world. He knew what he was doing. He knew a woman's body as well as his own, so under the circumstances she couldn't agree. Eventually he would feel her enlarging belly and he would know. Then his professed interest would change into loathing because he would think she'd set him up; that she had gotten pregnant on purpose.

"I suppose we could talk."

* * *

One Night with the Texan is part of
Lauren Canan's the Masters of Texas series.

Dear Reader,

I have always had a fascination with history—
especially the historical events that happened in my
own backyard. I couldn't count the number of hours
I've spent searching for artifacts predating the Civil
War. It was with this in mind that *One Night with the
Texan* came to be.

This is the second book in the Masters of Texas
series. Meet Cole Masters, Chance's older brother.
Just when Cole is about to begin building a complex
that's been years in the making, an archaeologist
shows up with a court order telling him to cease and
desist for ninety days—effectively bringing Cole's
multimillion-dollar project to a screeching halt.

Dr. Tallie Finley is on a mission. The day before
her grandmother died she handed Tallie a very old
map showing the location of the first tribe of their
people, who were never recorded in history. She
wants Tallie to find the original encampment and
ensure their people are documented. The only
problem with that request—it puts her at odds with a
stubborn, arrogant, gotta-have-it-his-way billionaire
who owns the land and has made it clear he wants
her gone. What she doesn't immediately realize is
they've met before. In a one-night stand two months
prior. And she's carrying his child.

Let the games begin.

Lauren Canan

LAUREN CANAN

ONE NIGHT WITH THE TEXAN

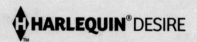

HARLEQUIN® DESIRE

Recycling programs
for this product may
not exist in your area.

ISBN-13: 978-0-373-83827-1

One Night with the Texan

Printed in U.S.A.

Lauren Canan has always been in love with love. When she began writing, stories of romance and unbridled passion flowed through her fingers onto the page. Today she is a multi-award-winning author, including the prestigious Romance Writers of America Golden Heart® Award. She lives in Texas with her own real-life hero, four dogs and a mouthy parrot named Bird.

She loves to hear from readers. Find her on Facebook or visit her website, laurencanan.com.

Books by Lauren Canan

Harlequin Desire

Terms of a Texas Marriage
Lone Star Baby Bombshell

Masters of Texas

Redeeming the Billionaire SEAL
One Night with the Texan

Visit her Author Profile page at Harlequin.com, or laurencanan.com, for more titles.

One

Cole Masters descended the steps of the hotel after his business meeting, bodyguards in tow, and walked toward the waiting limo that would take him to the airport and back to Dallas. The deal he was here to finalize had gone without a hitch. He'd actually been hoping the other party would voice some objections, stir things up a bit. But it had gone down as just another dull and boring merger.

Cole stopped and looked around him. The late-afternoon sun felt good on his face. New Orleans. The Big Easy. It had been years since he'd ventured into the French Quarter with all its laughter and music, but he remembered it fondly. Suddenly something snapped inside and he walked to the waiting car.

"Find out where there's a thrift store. Something like Goodwill."

"Sir?"

"Just do it, please."

The driver disappeared inside the car and returned minutes later with an address.

"Excellent. Can you take me there?"

"Yes, sir."

"Gene, you and Marco are dismissed," he said to the security detail. "The plane is waiting in Concourse D. Use it and fly home."

"Mr. Masters, I don't know if this is such a good idea."

"It'll be fine. Have the pilot back here by tomorrow afternoon."

Cole got into the limo. "Let's go shopping," he told the driver and they were off, leaving the two bodyguards standing at the edge of the street staring after him as though he'd lost his mind. And maybe he had. He wanted to be wild, live in the moment, free of obligations to anyone or anything. Blend in with the other pedestrians and enjoy the few hours he'd allotted himself.

He was tired. Tired of the yes-men who would agree with anything he said. Tired of people using him. Tired of the same corporate demands, the same schemes. He'd grown weary of knowing what questions would be asked and knowing the answers before words ever left the person's mouth. He was especially tired of being hostage to the family's business negotiations. The image he was required to maintain had come to feel like a chain around his neck. He couldn't free himself from it. He couldn't get a reprieve. Consequently he knew he had become hard and bitter. He heard words come from his mouth he didn't recognize as his own. People were starting to distance themselves from him and he didn't blame them. Cynical, suspicious, contemptuous; he sometimes saw himself through others' eyes and didn't like what he'd become. As the CFO of a successful 8.2 billion-dollar family conglomerate, he took no pride in his accomplishments.

After purchasing jeans, T-shirt, jacket and a pair of scuffed shoes, he dismissed the driver, changed his clothes and hit the streets where hopefully no one would recognize him and subsequently no one would ask anything of him. He would let his soul get lost in the music and the ambience that is only New Orleans.

The man looked every bit as daunting up close as he had from a block away. The hard features of his wickedly handsome face bore the stamp of experience: a complete awareness of the world around him and those in it. Even in the increasing darkness, illuminated only by small twinkle lights strung over the outside tables at the bistro, that much was obvious. The dark, chocolate-brown hair with lighter highlights seemed to accent the golden brown of his eyes. Eyes that tempted her to look closer. To come closer without any rational thought of the consequences.

His lips were full, sensuous, made for seduction.

She couldn't stop herself from imagining what it would be like to feel them moving over her own; feel his hands caress her body as the heat between them intensified. His skills in bed would be amazing. How she knew, she couldn't answer. But she knew.

Tallie Finley sensed he would be a formidable opponent. He was tall, powerfully built, dressed in a pair of jeans that had seen better days, a black T-shirt with some faded design on the front and a black jacket that appeared too large—an amazing feat when one considered the breadth of his shoulders. He impressed her as a man who had at one time owned the world and lost it. But not without a fight.

"What's next?" Kate "Mac" McAdams asked, polishing off the last of her glass of wine.

"Beads. We cannot go home without earning our beads," Ginger Barnes stated.

Leaving the stranger behind—again, because it seemed that everywhere she went tonight, he was there—Tallie followed her two friends out to Bourbon Street to experience the "Beads for Boobs" tradition, knowing it was one she would pass up.

Once they'd climbed the stairs to their second-story hotel room, Tallie made her way out to the balcony railing and looked down into the crowds below. The people in the adjacent apartment were already vying for their beads. Guys on the street held up ropes of the shiny multicolored necklaces for display, tempting the girls on the balcony to remove their tops and show all.

Street musicians vied with the jazz and R & B

pouring out the open doors of bar-and-grills in a manner you'd think would clash. But not here. Not in this amazing city. The air was full of laughter, drunken wolf whistles, woots and cheers, the flamboyant colors of the clothes and the scent of spices and food cooking over open grills. It was a world like none other and Tallie was front and center. She would miss it when it was time to leave and begin her new research appointment in Texas.

"Don't just stand there," called Ginger, her closest friend and roommate for the past six years during college and grad school. "You've got 'em, girl. Use 'em!"

"Right on," Mac encouraged. She made up the third of the trio. She'd flown to the Big Easy just to celebrate with her best friends.

"I don't think so," Tallie refused. "But don't let me stop you."

"Oh, you won't," Mac answered with a wink. "If you're chicken, I'll go first. I've got to get some of those beads."

"You do know you can buy them in the local stores?"

"Yes, but where's the fun in that?"

With her hips gyrating to the heavy beat reverberating off the walls, the blonde teasingly danced her way out to the balcony edge and began to unfasten her shirt, button by button. The crowd below began to clap and yell even louder.

If you blinked, you missed it. But apparently it was enough because men quickly threw strings of various colored beads up to her. Tallie watched in disbelief as Ginger did the same thing. Then both her friends looked at her.

Tallie shook her head. "I'm gonna pass. This just isn't my thing. And frankly, I'm surprised at the two of you doing something this…bizarre."

"Do you mean to tell me you're going out in the world—about to start your new career with a Ph.D. in your pocket—and you're going to let this amazing memory slip by?" Ginger had to yell to be heard over the crowd and the music. She giggled and downed the rest of her drink.

Tipsy. They were both tipsy and headed to full blown smashed.

"That's exactly what I'm saying," she laughed. No way would she ever be so intoxicated she would shake her boobs in front of a hundred people from a second-story balcony. What had gotten into her studious, straight-laced friends? She could understand blowing off steam after all the hard work they'd done to get their degrees, but still. "Come on. There has to be someplace we haven't been yet." She led the others down the stairs back to the street. "I feel like dancing."

"I could do some dancing," Ginger agreed. "Give me a sultry, sexy tune anytime. Here—" Ginger looped several strands of beads over Tallie's head "—you gotta have some finery if you want to be asked to dance."

"She's right," Mac added as she draped more

strands of beads around Tallie's neck. "Now it looks like we're all daring and ready to get down."

Get down? Tallie could only imagine.

"Anybody have a suggestion? I'm guessing this being a Friday night, the better pubs and lounges are full," Ginger sighed.

"I saw lines of people waiting to get in a couple of places on our way back here," Mac added. "But there has to be someplace we can go."

"Wait, wait. I heard some people talking at the bistro about a place on the outskirts of the Quarter they thought was good. The Gator Trap Bar and Grill. It's on Bourbon Street down toward St. Ann. I want to try a drink they mentioned called the Horny Crock." Ginger giggled. "Or the Swamp Itch."

"That sounds bad," the other two chimed in.

"I didn't name them. But I could sure drink one. Or two!"

After agreeing on the next destination, they refreshed their drinks at a street vendor and headed down Bourbon.

If there was a bar in New Orleans moodier and more atmospheric than the Gator Trap, Tallie couldn't imagine what it must be like. The place was dark. There were candles on each table and lights heralding the yuletide season that had ended five months ago still hung over the large mirror behind the bar. They provided the only light. The soulful sax, trumpet, piano and bass coming from the quartet in the back of the room pulled you in.

While Ginger and Mac headed for the ladies' room Tallie slipped onto a seat at the bar.

"What can I get you?" the bartender asked as he removed two dirty glasses from in front of her and wiped the countertop. Tallie gave her order.

"Make that two," said a man to her right as he tossed some bills on the counter. "I couldn't say I've experienced New Orleans without sampling a Swamp Itch."

Laughing, Tallie swung around, her eyes growing wide as she recognized the mysterious man she'd been seeing at various places most of the evening. His golden eyes were gleaming with humor as he acknowledged her. "We seem to have a lot in common."

"You mean like the aquarium?" The first time she'd seen him was as she was leaving the aquarium.

"And the artists on Jackson Square."

"Yes. Some were brilliant, didn't you think? We didn't make it to the paddle boats or the zoo," she said. "Did we?" She wondered if he had gone there.

"No, we didn't. We'll have to save those for next time."

His voice was deep and crusty and well over the line to absolutely sexy. As their drinks were placed before them, he offered a toast. "Here's to new experiences."

"To new experiences." Tallie grinned. This entire evening had definitely been that and more. She'd gone to school here but had never let herself get drawn into the nightlife. Money was tight and she'd taken her studies seriously. Archeology wasn't just a degree for her. It was a passion.

Ginger had been right in her speculation that the drinks would be good here. Between the warm, humid air filling the room and the man's close presence, Tallie all but guzzled the entire glass.

"Two more," the man said, holding up some money. He laid it on the counter and looked back at Tallie. "Dance with me."

It wasn't a question. But when he took her hand in his much larger one she didn't protest. He led her to the small dance floor, placed her hands on his shoulders and held her close with both arms around her. As expected, he was all hard muscle and iron strength. She was five seven, but the top of her head barely reached his collarbone. Rather than talk, he seemed content to hold her close and move to the soulful music. It worked for her.

She caught a glimpse of Ginger and Mac as they passed by. Both grinned and winked, giving her a thumbs-up. After three songs her mystery man led her back to the bar where their freshened drinks awaited. Like before, she wasted no time emptying her glass.

When the bartender approached, the man ordered for both of them. In French. "You'll like this drink. It's a specialty of the house."

And it was delicious.

"So, do you live here?" she asked, mesmerized by the way his Adam's apple moved when he swallowed his drink. Was there anything not sexy about this guy?

"No. I live…in various places. No one place I'd call home."

"Oh," she replied. "That's sad."

"Sad? You think it's sad to live all over the world?"

"I think its fine to travel on occasion, but you need a home base. At least, I would. A special place you long to return to. Somewhere you can kick off your shoes, turn off the phone, sleep in your own bed and know you're…well…home." Tallie patted his arm. "But don't worry. You'll get through the hard times and find a home. I guarantee it."

"I'll take your word for it." He pursed his lips as though he found her remark funny.

She finished her drink and he ordered two more. "Where is it you call home?"

"Texas. Far northeast. That's where I grew up, where my family lives. I've been going to school at Tulane. In the morning I head home."

The band kicked off another song just as the bartender set the two new beverages on the counter. The sexy stranger watched in obvious amusement while she took a sip. "This is really, really good."

"I'm glad you like it," he said, standing. "Ready?"

"Yes."

The tune was slow, moody and the perfect tempo. He once again enclosed her in his powerful arms and she rested her head against his shoulder and swayed to the music. She could smell his essence, feel the

heat of his body. His hands moved up and down her
back, easing her still closer. Then he cupped her
face, brushing her hair back over her shoulders. She
couldn't see much in the dim light, but what she saw
was mesmerizing. His amber eyes seemed to glow,
but it was his lips that beckoned her. What must it
be like to kiss him?

Before the thought could leave her mind he lowered his head and his lips covered hers, warm, gentle, enticing.

Tallie was struck by the soft pliability of his
mouth, which was a complete contrast to the hard-
muscled body that pressed against her. But the kiss
was so brief she wondered if she'd imagined it. He
watched her as though looking for any sign she
didn't want to be kissed. She smiled, conveying a
silent approval. Apparently satisfied, he again bent
his head toward her. "You are so beautiful." His
breath was warm against her ear, sending shivers
racing across her skin. He returned to her mouth
and drew his tongue across her lips, enticing them to
open. Without conscious thought, she complied. His
tongue swept inside her mouth, deep and decisive.
He tasted of a dark spice, with a hint of the drink
they'd been enjoying, along with his own unique all-
male flavor, and she couldn't get enough.

She gently suckled his tongue and he moaned,
filling her mouth, going deep, as though he needed
to taste all she had to offer. Tallie had never been
kissed like this, with such expertise, such blatant
sexuality. It was so far removed from the stilted

good-night kisses she'd experienced in the past, and she knew now that she'd never really been kissed. Too soon, his lips left hers as he licked and kissed across her jaw to her earlobe. Then, as if he had no choice, his mouth returned to hers and she was once again sinking in a dizzying storm of emotions as his lips, his scent, the feel of his skin and the power of his body, consumed all rational thought.

He made a slight adjustment and she felt his desire press against her belly. Her body's natural instinct was to push against him. In response, he moaned, low and deep. His lips again covered hers in another deep, drugging kiss laced with pure fire.

The way he held her and kissed her was so primal, so captivating. She could sense his strength even though he held it at bay. He gave her no time to think as he returned to her lips, both hands cupping her face as he pushed any other thought from her mind. Then one hand came around her waist, holding her close while the other entangled in her hair, drawing her head back as the kiss deepened, intensified. She gripped the front of his open jacket and held on as the feel of hot lava ran through her veins, pooling below her belly.

It was amazing how their bodies fit together so perfectly. Her breasts pressed against his broad chest. His muscular thighs and his erection pushed hard against her. A cloud of heat surrounded her and sexual instincts overtook logic as she moved against him. Had they stopped dancing? Were they still on the dance floor?

Tallie didn't want to open her eyes for fear it might break the spell.

Two

The world around them disappeared. Tallie knew only the warmth and taste of this stranger's lips and tongue and the incredible way he made her feel. His scent was pure male. His actions screamed experience. Lots of it. And she never wanted this to end. There was something in his voice, in his body language, that drew her to him. Maybe it was a rush of pheromones? Whatever the cause, it was definitely past time to take some risks in her admittedly sheltered life. This man looked like he'd seen both the worst life had to offer and the best. What tremendous hardships had he weathered? No home. Old clothes that didn't fit. Every time she'd seen him over the course of the evening he'd been alone. She didn't want him to be alone.

Slowly their lips parted and his strong arms surrounded her, holding her close.

"The music stopped," he said, his voice deep and raspy. "I could use some fresh air. How about you?"

When she nodded her agreement he took her by the hand and headed for the door. Outside he continued to lead her down the worn sidewalk, where they were surrounded by revelers who didn't seem to have a care in the world.

Tallie hated for the evening to end. This was one night she would never forget. "Thanks for dancing with me. I love to dance and don't get to do it very often."

"It was my pleasure. Let me walk you back to your hotel."

"Thank you. It's this way." She pointed then frowned. "Oh. No, it's that way." She looked back at him and detected humor in his eyes. "I can't remember how I got here. But I'll figure it out. You don't have to stay out here because of me."

"What's the name of your hotel?"

Surely she could remember. But she finally had to admit she didn't have a clue. "It's something in French." She absently chewed her bottom lip, shook her head and once again looked around where they stood.

"How about coming to my place? We can have a bite to eat, make some tea and I'm sure your memory will come back."

The delicious drinks were clouding her mind.

Even outside in the evening air, her head was still spinning.

"You know you really are a very nice man."

"Don't think I'm too nice," he said, taking her hand and leading her down the darkened street. "Not when I have a beautiful woman in my arms."

Since she had never been considered beautiful in her life, his words struck her as funny. Tallie couldn't stop the giggle from leaving her throat.

She felt light on her feet, as though she was floating on air. Then she realized that he'd picked her up and was carrying her in his arms. After that, everything was a blur. A bell dinged and doors opened in front of them. She rested her head on his shoulder thinking what an incredible night it had been.

She caught a glimpse of his face through the darkening shadows. So very male. The deep indentions on both sides of his mouth seemed to make him that much more delicious. But it was those golden eyes that consumed her.

She had a vague realization that they were in a private apartment, although there was no light in the room. He set her on her feet.

"I'll put that tea on," he said and stepped back from her.

Tallie stepped forward, her hands running down the front of his shirt. Standing on her tiptoes, she placed her lips on his. The passion between them surged.

He pulled back. "Be very careful of what you ask

for, darlin'. You're playing with fire and you're likely to get burned. I don't do relationships."

"What do you do?" Tallie was acting out of character, but it felt good. For the first time in her life she was actually flirting with a man.

"I think I'd better make the tea."

"Do you really want tea?"

He stared at her in silence. She had her answer and suddenly she felt foolish. She could feel the blush crawl up her neck and cover her face. "I'm not looking for a relationship, either," she said, turning away and picking up her purse. "And I know when I'm not wanted. Thanks again for the dance. Good night."

Tallie walked toward the door.

Before she could open it he was in front of her, ensuring the door remained closed.

"Where are you going?"

"Back to my hotel. I'm just having a little trouble remembering where it is." The humiliation burned inside like acid, acting as anti-venom for the passion she'd felt only moments ago. It stopped her from doing anything else stupid but couldn't reverse the damage already done. She should never have accepted his offer to dance. "I'll get a taxi."

"And tell them to go where?"

He took her purse from her hand and tossed it behind them on the sofa. Then he picked her up again and carried her to a bedroom, setting her down gently next to the bed. His lips found hers again in a smoldering kiss. She was dimly aware he was unbuttoning her blouse. She sensed coolness against her back and a freedom from any restrictions and hazily realized he had removed her blouse and her bra. She ran her arms across the cool, silken sheets. The scent of incense hung heavy in the air around them. With one fluid movement his jacket and T-shirt hit the floor and she heard the zipper on his jeans.

His body was magnificent and Tallie knew they were about to cross a line, one that seemed to be growing blurrier by the second. If she didn't say no immediately, he was going to make love to her.

As if sensing her apprehension, he raised his head, watching her through the dim glow of the subdued lighting, his eyes almost black with desire.

Her gaze moved over his face, finally coming to rest on his mouth.

"Are…are you married?" she whispered, running one finger across his bottom lip.

"No." He lightly bit the tip of her finger before sucking it gently into his mouth and then releasing it. A shot of pure heat speared through her. "I'm going to make love to you. But I need to know you're okay with this."

"Yes," she said. More than he might ever know. Any other time her timidity would step in and she wouldn't think of admitting such a thing. She wasn't sure if it was the alcohol she'd consumed or the man.

"I was hoping you would say that."

Bracing his weight on both his arms and one knee, he hovered over her, kissing her cheek and trailing his teeth across her jawline, causing a surge of heat to flood her lower regions.

Oh, yes. She was very sure she wanted this. To hell with caution and rational thinking. She reached out to touch his face and felt the coarse five-o'clock shadow. In his arms she ached, overwhelmed with the feeling she was incomplete, needing him to make her whole. He kissed the palm of her hand then proceeded to suckle her fingers one finger at a time. His heavy body settled over hers. She felt his erection, hard and unyielding against her core, and heard him emit a deep growl. Pure liquid heat ran through her veins and Tallie was lost. Her head fell back on the pillow as the world spun. She pressed against him out of pure instinct, needing more, her body demanding it.

This incredible man was about to make love to her. And she was going to let him. A complete stranger. She'd gone around the bend to insanity. She inhaled a deep breath, the need for him destroying the last of her common sense. Her body was on fire. Was she dreaming? Or was this her prince charming in disguise? In this moment it didn't matter. She was his. And she really couldn't imagine anything better.

He stripped her of her jeans and panties in short order. She heard his own jeans hit the floor and then he was back. The strands of gold, blue and red beads fell around her breasts. They felt cold compared to the heat that was raging through her. His hand slid down over her stomach and farther, testing to ensure she was ready for him. He adjusted his body over hers. She knew a moment of panic as she noted the immense size of him. She wouldn't be able to compete with his overpowering strength. She suddenly felt small and helpless as she realized she would have no control.

"This is your last chance to say no," he told her, as if reading her mind, his voice both deep and hoarse with emotion. His breathing was shallow. She felt the blunt end of his sex positioned at her core. "Once I'm inside you, I can't guarantee I'll be able to stop."

All Tallie could do was nod her head and hope her instincts about this man were right. She wanted this. Just once in her life she wanted to be with a man who could give her the experience she'd previously only heard about. Just once.

In what seemed to be slow motion, his lips again descended, finding and suckling her breast. His large hand kneaded the other, gently pinching her swollen nipple, making her arch her back as she swelled under his touch. Then he cupped her head in his hands, as though holding her where she needed to be. She inhaled the raw scent of him, lost in the heady potency that surrounded him. She felt her body relax, her mind clear of all thought, accepting what was to come without any thought of denying him what she knew he was about to take. The breath left her lungs on a sigh as the world grew dark and he was all that existed.

He pushed inside and the last remnant of her mind disappeared. Even though he went slowly, careful not to hurt her, she'd never been filled to such a degree. She hadn't realized how muscular he was; how much bigger his body felt against hers. She inhaled a shuddering breath. As if understanding, he stopped.

"Take it easy, hon," he whispered against her ear. "Just let yourself relax."

Seconds passed and the pressure turned to incessant need. When she pushed against him, he began to move. Deeper. Harder. It sent her spiraling and, almost instantaneously, with a cry, she exploded. He held her close, encouraging, speaking words that made her climax go on and on.

She heard the foil packet being ripped open and seconds later he returned to her. He raised her hands above her head and kissed her neck and breasts as he entered her and once again began to move. This time more forcefully, almost urgently, his strength obvious in the way he held her; the way he took her. He pounded into her until it was both too much and yet not enough, bringing her to the edge then backing off, over and over until she wanted to scream.

She whimpered her frustration.

"What is it you want, sweetheart?"

"Please," she whispered, straining against him. "It's so hot."

The excessive heat between her legs burned and there was only one person who could give her relief.

He began to move again and this time it was with one intention. She became separated from reality, her body one with his. She couldn't open to him enough as he fulfilled her every need, bringing her to orgasm then joining her. The groan he made as he found his release was the sexiest sound she'd ever heard.

He fell to her side and pulled her next to him, her head on his shoulder. She experienced the feeling of a warm, cozy cocoon, his heavy arms around her, holding her close. Later in the night she was awakened and, once again, knew mindless passion. Then, once again, she slept.

"Tallie!" a woman's voice called out, followed by a knock on the door. "Tallie, where are you?"

She opened her eyes and looked around the room at the strange surroundings. "I'm in here," she responded in a sleepy voice. The door opened and Ginger and Mac sailed into the room.

"When you never came back to the hotel, we got pretty worried," Mac said, walking around the room. The soft morning sunlight attempted to enter through the edges of the lush, thick draperies. "Then early this morning some man called from your phone and left a message saying you were okay and where we could find you. He must have seen our panicky texts."

Tallie sat up, immediately realizing she had on no clothes. Covering herself with the sheet, she rubbed her eyes and yawned. "What time is it?"

"Almost eight, you wicked, lucky girl." Ginger smiled and winked at Tallie. "Who would have ever thought that, of the three of us, Miss Quiet Mouse would be the one to get lucky?"

"Eight…in the morning?"

"Yep. We need to get back to the hotel and pack. Our flight is at noon," Mac reminded her. "And you will have two hours to tell us every naughty luscious tidbit of last night's little escapade." She tossed Tallie her clothes. "And this is one you're not getting out of."

"Are you going to see him again?" Ginger asked. "I couldn't see him very well in the bar. Is he cute?"

Tallie didn't know what to say. Cute was not an adjective she would use to describe him. Sixteen-year-old boys were cute. This was a man in every sense of the word. As far as his looks, she hadn't gotten a very good look at him—everywhere they met, it had been dark. Would she recognize him again? Possibly. Possibly not. "I would have to say he was handsome," she told Ginger. "And definitely sexy."

"Yeah, we kinda got that."

"He had a sexy voice when he called," Mac added.

As Tallie moved to get out of bed she felt sore in places she never knew she had. She smiled to herself. He had been an exceedingly patient and proficient lover. Amazing. Just as she put her feet on the plush carpet a sight caught her eye. A folded store receipt. On the back was written "You are the best. Thanks, C—"

"What is that?" Ginger asked.

"Did he write you a note?" Mac asked, walking toward the bed. "I hope you got his phone number!"

Still staring at the receipt in her hand she slowly

shook her head, still stunned that she'd lost all control last night.

"I don't even know his name."

Three

Three months later

Tallie looked around her at the open farmland extending as far as her eyes could see. A river snaked through the golden, knee-high wheat, feeding huge trees that grew sporadically in giant clumps near its edge. An old trapper's shack that a sneeze could probably blow down sat under the branches of a giant, towering oak. To the east were cliffs, their dark red composite a vivid contrast to the white-gold of the wheat. Dark impressions on the face of the cliffs gave indication of caves, which could have at one time been home to ancient people.

It had taken her an enormous effort to get the huge bulldozers and other machinery to shut down on this site. But she'd finally ascertained which man was the head of this operation and waved the court document under his nose. Now, with the motors of the huge machines turned off, only the sound of the wind blowing through the wheat and the occasional call of a bird remained.

Somehow in this mass of timber, cliffs and cultivated soil that went on for miles she was supposed to find confirmation that an ancient people had, at one time, existed. A tribe of Native Americans never referenced in any record book in history. Never mentioned by scholars or spoken of in the homes of the people. Except one: her paternal grandmother's. The day before she'd died.

When a person so dear to her heart asked Tallie to find her people and, with trembling hands, opened her palm and dropped a tiny token into hers, Tallie had no other option but to promise she would do as asked. A sense of calm had overtaken her *ipokini* and, with a smile, she'd handed Tallie one other item: a doeskin about two feet square, rolled and tied with a braid of leather.

On the inside of the doeskin was a crude, hand-drawn map. One large area, marked in faded red powder, must relate to what her grandmother had asked her to find. It encompassed an area from a river on the west where the water washed the roots of a massive oak tree to just beyond cliffs to the east. At various points inside the red circle were rudimentary images similar to those found in caves. A horse. A deer. A warrior with a lance. A teepee village. At the top, a cryptic design indicated mountains. Across the bottom the word *Oshahunntee*. The tribe of no existence. Like many of the words taught by her grandmother, it was also unknown to all but a few.

Her *ipokini* was not a wealthy woman. Her gold was encased in a heart as big as Texas and spread among all the people she'd helped for almost one hundred years. For her to give Tallie something that must have been so special to her was a great honor. Tallie had promised her then—and in her heart now—that she wouldn't let her down.

She had been surprised when her boss, the chief curator at the museum where she'd worked the past three months, not only okayed her request to do this search but had, in fact, become quite excited when she'd showed him the map. Instead of making her take a leave, Dr. Sterling had endorsed it as an approved dig for the museum, though Tallie would have to cover her own personal expenses. Dr. Sterling had even been able to point her to the part of Texas the map seemed to describe. Now, with the court's backing to explore the site, only one thing might stand between her and discovery. She was pregnant.

Dr. Sterling had voiced his concern about her condition and made her promise to check in regularly. He couldn't spare another associate to send with her and had made it clear she would be on her own. She'd convinced him she was fine. And she was. Or soon would be. Beginning her third month of pregnancy, she was almost over the morning sickness. At least, she hoped so.

Discovering she was pregnant from her night in New Orleans had been a life-changing moment. Her memories of the encounter were so hazy, it was almost as if she'd been in a blackout. But she was left with a very real reminder of what had happened. She had no hope of finding the father, and initially, her dreams of the future had gone out the window. She couldn't imagine traveling the world on archeological expeditions with a baby. Yet as the idea of having one settled into her mind and filled her heart, she made peace with it. Other single mothers worked and raised their children. She could, too. Admittedly, she would have to halt travel to remote sites until the baby was old enough, but just because she didn't have a regular nine-to-five didn't mean she'd have to throw away years of study just to be a mother.

But right now she would concentrate on the present and take the future one step at a time. She was healthy and happy and determined to find the proof of the lost tribe as she'd promised her grandmother she would. At least, she had to try.

A chill went down her spine at the thought that the lost tribe might actually prove to have existed. But why had her grandmother waited until she was dying to tell her? And where had the map been all these years? She'd spent a lot of time at her *ipokini*'s house as a child and had never seen it or anything like it. Tallie could only suppose her grandmother had her reasons and all she could do now was accept that some things would never be explained.

Clutching the court-issued injunction in her hand, she took another look around. The paperwork required the owner of the property to halt all operations for ninety days so that she could search for relics. She would concentrate on the present and take the future one step at a time.

Suddenly the wind kicked up, blowing her long hair in every direction. She fought to catch it at the back of her head and then pulled a band from the pocket of her jeans and secured it in a rough knot on her crown. The sound of a helicopter in the distance shattered the silence. It was coming toward her and not wasting any time, soon landing a safe distance from where she stood between the old trapper's hut and the river. She didn't have to be told who it was. Cole Masters, billionaire eight-times-over and owner of this land, had arrived. Dr. Sterling had mentioned she might receive some resistance from this man, whose reputation for doing things his way preceded him.

The man who emerged from the chopper was big. Broad shoulders, his biceps bulging beneath the rolled-up sleeves of the white-silk dress shirt. A blue tie had been loosened at the neck to accommodate the unbuttoned top of his shirt. Honey-brown eyes were emphasized by dark lashes. His short, dark brown hair and his thick beard gave him the look of a warrior. His chiseled jaw was set for a fight. His full lips were drawn into a line of disapproval and those eyes were fixed on her as he marched to where she stood. So this was the great Cole Masters. Alive and in person.

In spite of her professional approach to matters such as these, the closer he came, the more she felt her years of study and experience fading to nothing. On that realization, she took a deep breath and concentrated on why she was here. This dig was a one-shot attempt to prove something incredible. She wouldn't allow herself to be swayed by his sex appeal or intimidated by his rumored bitterness and arrogance. She'd somehow maintain the professional attitude the situation called for.

"Cole Masters," he introduced himself, extending his hand.

"Dr. Tallie Finley, archaeologist with the North Texas Natural History Museum," she said as she accepted his hand. It was twice the size of hers and exceedingly warm. A slight electric current tingled between their grips, traveling some distance up her arm. She could tell by his frown he'd felt it, too. She quickly withdrew her hand.

"It's *you*." His brows raised in surprise and his demeanor became less in your face.

"Ah…yes. I'm me and I'm guessing this is what you want to see." Something about him seemed vaguely familiar but she couldn't quite place him.

She handed him the court document. "It allows an intrusive and extensive survey of the area indicated on the map as presented to the court."

"*You* are Dr. Finley?"

Something had suddenly removed the harsh tone from Mr. Masters's voice and replaced it with a slight hint of congeniality. Because she didn't know what had caused the change, she was more off kilter than when she'd initially faced his hostility. Good grief. Had she failed to button her blouse? Was she wearing the oatmeal she'd had for breakfast?

"I am."

"Dr. Finley…" he said again, and handed the paper back to her. He cleared his throat. "Do you see that heavy equipment over there?" He swung around and nodded at the bulldozers, cement trucks and other pieces of large equipment she couldn't name. "We are in the middle of a project. The planning alone has taken years. These guys are here today to pour the foundations, all twenty-five of them. As you can see, the roughed-in plumbing is already installed. How are we supposed to do our work if you're in the same area looking for whatever you think might be there?"

Her eyes were drawn to his lips. So full. So enticing. She swallowed hard. She again had that vague feeling of having met this man before but the only face that came to mind was the mysterious stranger who had seduced her. No way could the two men be the same.

"I understand this might be an inconvenience for you, Mr. Masters. But the reason I'm here is equally important. Possibly more so." He drew back, shaking his head. "What I'm seeking could potentially be under the spot where you plan to pour concrete, which would be a problem. If there are artifacts there, they could be damaged by your construction. If you'll tell your workers to move their equipment out of my work area, I'll conduct my research as expeditiously as I can to get out of your way."

"That's it?" His eyes locked with hers and she felt a tingle run down her spine. Where had she seen those eyes before? Suddenly a feeling of deja vu ran rampant. "We halt our operation and get out of *your* way? On *my* land." His frustration was coming back. She could see the muscles in his jaw working overtime. Something about his voice touched a nerve. She'd swear she'd heard it before, which was ridiculous. She didn't run in the same circles as billionaires.

"I would assume the judge knew who owned this land when he signed the order. I would have to say he's probably not going to change his mind. If you should decide to take your case before a higher court, it would take longer than I'll be here." Unless she found proof an ancient civilization existed, which would make the ninety-day limit moot, but she would be throwing gas on the fire to bring that up now.

"Yeah. He knows me. And I know that judge. My attorneys will handle this."

"Of course. That's entirely your right." The man sure didn't mind throwing his weight around. She'd never seen a court-ordered, ninety-day search permit overturned. But to smile, as she wanted to do, might provoke him further. She fought the urge. Neither of them needed that. Just the fact that he was here and causing a delay was bad enough.

He called out to one of his men. "Harvey, this is Dr. Finley." His eyes flashed to hers then back to his foreman. "She has a map detailing an area in which she needs to work and has been given the authority to do so by the court. Temporarily. I want the area flagged. Call Michaels at the land surveyor's office, if need be."

Harvey didn't look at all convinced he could do as asked, but he wasn't going to tell his boss that. "Yes, sir."

"And you'll have to move the equipment. Find a rise, in case we get a storm, and make sure it's all outside of her...*work* area. The concrete trucks need to go back to Latham's Equipment." He received another nod from his foreman. "Just what is it, exactly, you're looking for, *Doctor*?" His hands rose to his hips. "Some kind of Indian relics?"

"Something like that." It was a heck of a lot more than that. But because of his in-your-face attitude, she was hesitant to enlighten him further. He wouldn't care and it was her experience the more a land owner knew, the worse they could make it for the archaeology team. "Actually, I'm looking for artifacts establishing my own family line. The recovery of such relics will be of great scientific value to the Native American Historical Society as well as to the National Historical Association. Do you keep cattle here? I need to know so I can take precautions if the answer is yes," she continued.

"No," he replied. "No cows or any other livestock allowed on this part of the property."

He stared at her. His eyes narrowed as he looked, really looked, at her face. He couldn't stop his eyes from roaming from her eyes and lips down her body, all the way to her toes. He ran one hand over his lower face as her identity confirmed in his mind. It hit him like a blow to his solar plexus. His expression changed to a smile he tried to hold in check.

Tallie Finley was the beautiful woman he'd spent the night with in New Orleans. No doubt.

Apparently she hadn't recognized him. Yet. He currently wore a beard and was dressed in a suit and tie. He was certain she had a completely different perspective of him now than she had then. But he knew her. He would never forget those beautiful, voluptuous curves, that stunning face, the long, silky, ebony hair and that deep Southern drawl.

She was the vision he'd dreamed about and thought about for almost three months. While striking, in the darkness her eyes hadn't been such a vivid green. Now they blazed emerald fire.

"Your eyes are so green." It just came out. And right now they were spitting green daggers.

She stared like he'd gone daft then turned away, suddenly angry. "Is the color of my eyes of great importance?"

"No. No. I just…it surprised me, that's all."

"Yeah, well, a lot of things surprise me."

Yeah, Cole thought. And she was going to face

a whopper of a surprise just around the corner. He would wait to see how long it took her to figure it out.

She reached up and pulled the band from her hair. With a quick shake and a finger-comb it was floating on the breeze like a dark, wispy cloud.

Damn, she was a beautiful woman. Tall and slender. Still a head shorter than his six foot four, she appeared both fragile and resilient. He had firsthand, intimate knowledge she possessed both those qualities. Her eyes demanded respect. Her hair was long, past her waist, and so black it looked blue under the direct sunlight. He could see the determination in her stance; in the way she carried herself. High cheekbones and those brilliant green eyes stood out in her slightly bronzed face. A man could get lost in those eyes. Easily. But he saw the determination in them. She wasn't here on a fool's mission. She would fight for the right to work on this dig and uncover evidence of her Native American ancestors' lost tribe. How did a man compete with something like that? *If* she was legit. If she was really here to find artifacts.

"Is there anything more I can do for you, Mr. Masters?"

He stepped toward her until less than a foot separated them. "That is the question."

He was close enough that he could feel the warmth of her body.

She stepped back. "If not, I need to get busy."

He'd never thought he would see her again, although he'd hoped to. He'd kicked himself a hundred times for not getting her name and contact information before he'd left that Saturday morning. He began to relax. With her hair piled up on top of her head at first and the green coveralls that hid every luscious curve, he was surprised he'd recognized her. But he had and she was here. His project was going to be delayed for a while but now it had a silver lining.

He could only stare as she began to work her locks into a long, silken braid. Suddenly it felt as though they were the only two people on earth. In this setting it wasn't hard to imagine. The sight caused every cell in his body to spring to readiness. A liquid heat ran rampant through him, pooling in his groin. It was New Orleans on steroids. And he wanted her until it hurt.

Images raced through his mind; images of her in bed, sheets tangled from their hot, sensual love-making. On her face were satisfaction and the need for more of him, which he gladly gave. Her ebony hair draped over his chest as he held her hot, damp body in his arms, fighting to slow his breathing. Tallie left the rest of the women he'd known in the dirt. How long until he could hold her in his arms again? There was no thought of never.

Cole took a deep breath and blew it out. He needed to push his wayward thoughts to the back of his mind and get away from this woman with all possible speed. Making a concentrated effort, he snapped himself out of the daydream. *Get a grip*.

"I—" He cleared his throat. "I'll leave you to your

work." He nodded, turned and walked back toward the chopper, his clarity of mind shot to hell.

He hadn't gone ten feet before he stopped and turned to face her. "Have you ever been to New Orleans, Dr. Finley?"

She squinted her eyes and tilted her head, no doubt finding the question odd.

"It's where I went to school. So, yes. I spent six years there. Why?"

He shrugged. "You just look like someone I knew once who lived there." He planted the seed. Now to see how long it would take her to come to figure things out.

A long moment passed between them before he turned toward the helicopter, boarded, started the massive engine, lifted off and flew away.

"Thanks for welcoming me to the neighborhood," she muttered to herself as she turned toward her old, battered Ford. What an odd man.

And she couldn't get over the fact that her mind was screaming, *You know him!* It was an absurdity. He traveled the world, was worth billions with a capital B, while she worked in the dirt and had barely a thousand bucks in the bank. Still…she couldn't seem to shake the feeling they had met before. And what was with that question about New Orleans? She'd gone to school there but she surely would remember if she had ever met him. She never ventured far from campus and knew very few that weren't associated with the college.

In fact, the only real outing she'd had was when she, Mac and Ginger had gotten together after graduation. She'd met a handsome stranger that night. But no way could that man have been Cole Masters. The stranger was nice and showed no arrogance at all. If the stranger had even one penny for every hundred thousand Masters had, he would be doing all right. He could even buy himself some new clothes. They were almost the same size. No doubt that's what kept bugging her. Pushing the thoughts from her mind she began to unpack the old Ford wagon. Maybe it would come to her eventually.

It took her a while to unpack. Most of her things could be stored inside the trapper's cabin. It was on the land covered by the court order, so she had no qualms using it. If Cole Masters didn't like it, she could always set up her tent. A closer inspection confirmed the one-room shack was sturdier than she'd originally thought. It contained an old wood-burning stove and a twin-size bed. The mattress, once white, was now the color of the dirt outside and so old it had been stuffed with peanut shells and cotton. There were holes in the roof and floor and the only window didn't have any panes. She had camped in worse. She just couldn't remember when. Her sleeping bag would provide some insulation and the rusty legs of the bed would keep her off the floor, so there was that at least.

She was used to roughing it, but her pregnancy added an extra wrinkle to the situation. Before she'd come here, her doctor had given her the green light—she was in excellent health and should be fine to do her job. But he'd warned her to take care of herself. The cabin would do for now, but she was going to have to keep a close eye on how she was feeling and make sure she didn't overdo it.

By the time she had unpacked most of her things, the bulldozers had been moved and an area had been marked off by little red flags. It was actually a larger area than she'd first imagined. She would have to thank Mr. Masters for that the next time he came snooping, which, if he was like other land owners, should be in about three days.

Tallie eyed the area to determine the best place to start. Over toward the cliffs, she decided. She would map out a grid and go from there.

She returned to her car for the last of the gear. Her old tent was on the bottom of a pile of equipment. She probably should drag it out and spend some time patching the rips and holes. She hadn't taken time to patch it after the last dig when the wind had blown it into a huge cactus patch. But she was anxious to start the dig. She would leave it for now and just use the old trapper's cabin. It was easier to ask for forgiveness than permission anyway. If Mr. Masters wanted her out of the ramshackle building, all he had to do was tell her.

She picked up the bolt of orange string, a handful of wooden stakes and a hammer, and chose a spot most favorable. She wouldn't finish before the sun set, but every step she could complete today would be one step closer to finding the proof of the lost tribe for her grandmother and the faster she could get back to the museum.

She wasn't used to working alone, but the silence was nice. She just hoped Masters found other things to occupy his time than coming out to bother her. She didn't need the veiled threats—or the sexual magnetism that made her heart speed up and her rational thinking, for which she was known, take a high dive off the nearest cliff.

With a sigh she hammered the first stake into the ground. Then another. By sunset she'd marked off an area of about one hundred and twenty square feet, and divided it into smaller sections. She'd been able to examine the first four grids. Tomorrow she would set up the sifting box and, with shovel in hand, she would be on her way to discovery. She hoped.

Grabbing her tools, she returned to the trapper's cabin, dropped the hammer and remaining stakes on the floor just inside the door and stared at the bed, such that it was. It was going to be a long night.

Cole walked from the helipad toward the house, still in disbelief, livid that Tallie Finley's dig was allowed to supersede his project and slow things to a crawl. It was ironic that on the day...*the day*...they were to pour the foundation she had received her permit from Judge Mitchell and shut Cole down. Unbelievable. Even more incredible was that he'd checked with his lawyers eight ways from Sunday and there was nothing he could do about the court order. The only silver lining was that he would have the opportunity to get to know this irresistible woman much better.

Since the day he'd left college his efforts had focused on company business, improving and doing his part to make Masters Corporation, LLC, one of the leading real-estate companies in Texas if not the entire United States. Days turned into nights that turned back into days as he'd worked. He'd flown countless miles, attended innumerable meetings. But it had always been for the family business; he'd never ventured out on his own. This project to build a world-class corporate retreat where Fortune 500 companies could send their executives for training and relaxation was special in that it was his. It was his chance to accomplish something important without company backing. He would prove his worth to his brothers and, more importantly, to himself. At the age of thirty-four he would finally be able to say, *I did that*. It wasn't about the money or acclaim. It was the sense of accomplishment and the pride.

The planning had taken years but the end was in sight. The announcement and a brochure detailing the project had gone out to the business leaders and entrepreneurs on almost every continent in the world. An invitation to tour the site had been sent to several prominent CEOs in the U.S. with the hope they would invest in the project. How uncharacteristically naive of him to think at this stage nothing would go wrong.

He'd never seen it coming. Just like before, when he'd found out about his ex-wife's cheating, he'd once again been caught with his pants down. If anyone had told him a month ago that a one-hundred-and-twenty-five-pound woman could shut down a multimillion-dollar project with a piece of paper and some orange string, he would have laughed in their face. He wasn't laughing now. He had to wonder if she was a part of a bigger plan by one of his corporate enemies to sabotage his project. If not, he had to be open to the possibility that she was working on her own in an attempt to gain some of his wealth. Did she know who he was and was she only acting a part? He'd learned three years ago just how deceptive a woman could be.

Even after the sheer hell he'd been through with his ex-wife, until today he thought he'd heard and seen it all. False pregnancy claims, varying attempts at blackmail. But claiming to look for some relic on the same spot as his future lodge was a new one. This must have taken some planning. How much was she being paid to sabotage his project and who was paying her to do it? What was the full game plan? Was she planning to fake an injury, as well? Had she set him up in New Orleans? Or was she legit?

As soon as he stepped into the house at the Circle M Ranch, he grabbed his cell and called the head of the security division at the home office in Dallas.

"Jonas? Yeah. I want someone checked out. I want to know when she lost her first baby tooth, the names of her friends in second grade, who she dated in college… I want you to turn over every rock no matter how small. Her name is Dr. Tallie Finley. She's supposedly an archeologist with the North Texas Natural History Museum. That's all I have."

"That should be plenty. I'll get right on it," said the voice on the other end of the line. "When I finish, I'll notify you by email?"

"Call me as soon as you have the full report. You can reach me at this number."

"Consider it done."

Cole hung up and slid his phone into his pocket. There had to be more to this than just a search for artifacts. No, she had to be after something more than a relic. It would be interesting to see what it was and how she went about trying to attain it.

For the first time in years, he thought of Gina. When they were newly married, he had trusted her, and she'd had his father's blessing. But less than a year into the marriage the warning signs had begun to appear. Lying. Disappearing for an afternoon or evening, money in her private account—tens of millions of dollars—vanishing at an alarming rate. His father's odd advice to not worry about it had sent Cole scurrying to the company's head of security, who'd provided a report that told it all. She was involved with another man. And she was pregnant. The father of the baby remained a mystery. Cole had had reason to doubt it was his.

But then tragedy had struck and that unborn baby had never gotten to see the world. Because he'd died with Gina the fateful night she'd spun out of control on a rain-soaked road, her car going over a steep embankment and exploding in flames at the bottom of a deep ravine. The night Cole had told her to get out.

There was just something about all the coincidences surrounding Dr. Finley's arrival that reminded him of his late wife's deception. Was Dr. Finley trying to play him, too? He damn sure didn't want to believe something bad about his new mystery woman, but neither did he intend to sit back and watch her destroy his plans.

Four

Three days after meeting her face to face, Cole still couldn't get over how Dr. Finley had taken over his land. He knew she'd settled into the trapper's cabin, and he was fine with that. The rough conditions in there would probably hasten her departure. He'd sent ranch hands out to spy on her at varying times. The reports were all the same. During the day, she worked. At night, she soaked in the river then disappeared into the little shack. They had to be missing something. Maybe she was sneaking around at night, looking for who knew what. He decided he would go out to assess the situation for himself.

Frustrated, Cole watched her through the lenses of his binoculars and confirmed what the ranch hands had reported. She worked from sunup to sun-

down, went for a dip in the cool waters of the river—
he had trouble taking his eyes off her voluptuous
curves—and finally trudged back to the old trapper's
cabin where she presumably slept through the night.
She was a damned hard worker, he'd give her that.
But after three days of this nonsense, it appeared
as though she'd found nothing, at least nothing she
cared to share with him, and his heavy equipment
still sat idle.

The next day his head of security called with the
findings about Dr. Finley. Nothing out of the or-
dinary and nothing he could use to get rid of her.
There was not one single thing she'd ever done that
was suspicious. No black mark against her. Not even
a gray one. She'd worked to put herself through
school. Her grades had been top-notch. She'd made
the dean's list in her junior and senior years of college before going for her master's degree then her
doctorate at Tulane University. Her mother's family was Irish. Her father was Choctaw. Her mother
taught seventh and eighth grade. Her dad had been
an archeologist before he was killed on a dig in Brazil four years ago. Dr. Finley had broken up with her
boyfriend, an English literature professor, a year
before.

But how could anyone in this day and age be that
squeaky clean? How was it possible?

He zeroed in on how she'd gone to Tulane. New
Orleans was a city Cole loved. In fact, the night he'd
spent there was the first time in years he'd taken the
opportunity to enjoy the city. Then, out of all the

people who swarmed into the French Quarter on that particular Friday night, he had ended up spending it with the most beautiful woman he'd ever set eyes on. That was one night, one memory, he would not soon forget. He would have never believed the next time he saw the woman she would be on his property, calling a halt to his pet construction project. It was uncanny. The chances were a billion to one. But as delighted as he was to see her again and this time to learn her name, he still would not wait ninety days to get his project back on track. Something had to give and it wouldn't be him.

Maybe if he talked to her, reined in his temper and kept it unemotional, just business, he could make her understand how many problems she was causing. And there was no time like the present. He jumped into a pickup and headed back to the site. He easily spotted her and walked to within a couple of feet of where she worked, moving the soil with a little brush. She glanced at him briefly in acknowledgment and continued to work, all but ignoring him. She was working about halfway through the grid, slowly, methodically, gently raking the dirt then brushing over anything that might be promising.

On hands and knees, she was leaning forward over her digging spot, her butt in the air. He wouldn't be a man if he didn't take another long look. She had a damn fine backside. Her hair was pulled up into a messy knot that made her look sexy as hell. Her face was smudged with dirt. He didn't know many women who would still look attractive in such a state. But it showed the commitment on Dr. Finley's part, which was something he had to admire.

"Dr. Finley, how are you doing today?"

"Just fine," she said, eying him suspiciously.

He cleared his throat. "I understand your dig, your search, is important to you." Admittedly he wasn't used to talking to someone's backside. "But the fact is, while you are out here playing with your rake in the dirt, I'm losing thousands of dollars a day."

"I'm sorry. That's too bad."

She didn't sound sorry. "Well, the thing is, I need to finish what I've started."

"If postponing your project is costing that much money, perhaps you should move it to another location," she suggested matter-of-factly, never taking her eyes off the section of ground she was working on.

"Impossible," he snorted. "I already have the plumbing roughed in. The forms are set. Other aspects of my project feed off of this location. It isn't that easy to just pick up and move."

"And if I find evidence next to one of your twenty foundations, that foundation will have to be torn out. You only have to stand down twelve weeks, maybe less." She looked up and caught his gaze. "Surely your business dealings have taught you that sometimes you don't get your way."

Cole could feel the anger rising in his chest. Even more frustrating, he couldn't escape the sheer physical pull of attraction he had for this woman.

"We have every reason to believe there may be remnants of an ancient civilization here," she continued. "I wasn't around several thousand years ago to warn them that in the twenty-first century someone would want to build...whatever you're building here."

She picked up a soft-bristle brush and began fanning over a small area.

"Dr. Finley," he mumbled. "There are museums full of paintings and crafts of all kinds. Why is this any different? What's so damned important that it's costing me a ninety-day delay? If what you're looking for is thousands of years old, what's another three months until you find them? It. Whatever you're searching for. Or is there something you're not telling me?"

Suddenly she dropped the little brush and stood. Pulling off her gloves, she slapped them against her jeans-covered leg. "I've already told you why you need to stop construction. Twice, if I recall. Why would you think I'm hiding something? What? Do you think I'm digging for gold? Some hidden Spanish treasure? A cache stashed by Jesse James?"

Now she was being snide.

"I assure you I'm not. Any of those things would be turned over to you immediately to do with as you pleased. Well, you and the IRS. And the longer you stand here harassing me, the longer I remain idle, causing further delays. Believe me when I say it's irritating for both of us."

"Fine." He glared at her. "Have it your way. But

don't expect any help from me or my employees." With that said, he turned and walked back to his truck.

A cool breeze came in through the broken window. She hoped it continued through the night. But as she got into the tiny bed she heard a scurrying of animal feet underneath it. Either rats or gophers. Maybe a raccoon. She quickly stepped to the opposite side of the cabin. "Go on. Shoo!" She beat against the rusted bed legs with a stick she'd found in the corner. Two skunks made their escape through the open cabin door, thankfully without releasing their odor. Bending over, she checked under the bed for any more night visitors. All clear.

With a shiver and a sigh, she went out to her Ford wagon in the hope she could find something to prop against the cabin door to keep it closed. She'd gone only a few steps when her foot got caught in a small indention in the ground, causing her to lose balance. She groped for anything that would keep her from falling and grabbed onto a low-hanging tree limb. But she immediately realized she'd become ensnared in a spider's web. The idea that the inhabitant might be looking for a new home somewhere inside her clothes slammed her panic button. As she frantically brushed at her clothing and hair, she heard a rustling of the underbrush a few feet away. It was then that she felt something crawling on her back. Under her shirt.

She screamed. There wasn't a lot in life that both-

ered her, but she'd been afraid of spiders since she
was a kid. In complete panic, she tore off her shirt
and began to brush at her back. Then something
moved just under the waistband of her jeans, heading
south. Another scream pierced the air as she frantically unbuttoned her pants and pushed them down
her legs. About the time they cleared her behind, she
lost balance, falling into a thick layer of last year's
autumn leaves. Rolling onto her back, she continued to kick and fight off the jeans that had bunched
around her ankles.

She'd just freed her feet when Cole appeared next
to her, coming down on one knee, a gun held with
both hands as he scanned the immediate area. "What
is it? What the hell is going on?"

"It's a…a spider."

"*What*?"

"A sss…spider," she sobbed, becoming aware that
she was sitting on the ground, almost naked, her
T-shirt hanging from a tree limb and her pants flung
to the side. She wasn't immediately sure what had
happened to her shoes.

He took a deep breath and blew it out. Shoving
the gun into the back of his jeans, he rose. "Stand
up," he ordered, catching her upper arm and pulling
her to her feet. Extracting a small flashlight from
his pocket, he checked her hair. Then she felt his
large hand move lightly across her shoulders and
down her back. Turning her to face him, he shone
the light on her face, down her neck and over her
breasts, which thankfully were still clad in her bra.

His face remained void of expression, even as he shined the light on her stomach and legs.

"I don't see anything," he said, a trace of annoyance in his tone. "How about you stay with me tonight? There's plenty of room."

He reached up and disentangled her shirt from the overhead branch, then picked up her jeans, shook them out and handed them back to her.

"Where are your shoes?"

"I... I'm not sure."

Without another word, he scooped her into his arms and began walking through the dried leaves in a direct line to his truck. Nestled against his broad chest, Tallie's arms instinctively came around his neck. He was so muscled, his chest and shoulders hard and unyielding. She'd only felt one other man with as much strength and power as this man had. Maybe that was the reason Masters reminded her of the guy in New Orleans. Like that other man, he moved gracefully, and carried her as though she weighed nothing at all. The heat rolled off his body, a warm caress against her back, arms and legs. He smelled faintly of hickory and something else she couldn't immediately define, but it was spicy and very appealing. And that was something she didn't need to notice. And there was still, at the back of her mind, the feeling she'd met this man before. But how was that even possible?

With the spider out of the picture and adrenaline no longer pumping through her veins, she felt more than a little foolish. She shouldn't let her phobias overrule her common sense.

A couple of feet from his truck, Cole paused. Tallie waited for the reprimand to come, for him to call her every kind of fool. But no words came.

She watched his eyes as he scanned her face, his intense expression a mixture of concern and something else she couldn't quite put a finger on. His lips, full and sensuous, were so close. For one crazy minute she thought he was going to kiss her and her breathing all but stopped. Then he turned away, pulled open the door and set her down on the passenger seat. Tallie sat, holding her shirt and jeans against her chest.

Within minutes Cole pulled up in the parking area near his house. They both got out of the truck and headed inside, past the enormous pool and waterfall.

The house was massive. The den was big enough to land one of his helicopters with room to spare. The walls were natural wood up to the third-story ceiling with an impressive natural-stone fireplace serving as the wall between the den and the kitchen.

Tallie followed him up a curving staircase. On the second floor they walked silently down a long hallway until he stopped and opened a door on the right. At that point, she lost the ability to describe the beauty of the room in front of her. It was carpeted in soft cream with walls painted to match; all of the accents, including the crown molding, internal doors and the fireplace mantel were mahogany.

The king-size poster bed with its intricate scrollwork matched perfectly.

"The towels are in the cabinet, as are the shampoos and bath salts. Come downstairs when you're finished. Andre is just starting supper, so take as long as you want."

She nodded, noticing the sparkle in his eyes that lit his handsome face. His full lips were pursed as though he was holding back a grin.

"Thank you," she murmured.

The bathroom boasted a huge whirlpool tub and a brown marble shower that could probably fit ten people. She had read about these thermostatic shower systems. This one had six shower heads plus a bench and steam jets that could turn it into a sauna. There were dual sinks in the same brown marble. The cabinets contained all the basic necessities: towels, washcloths, shampoo and soap. A lower drawer held an assortment of clean black and navy T-shirts, all size XXL.

Selecting one of the washcloths and a towel, she managed to turn on the water in the shower. Quickly stripping off her bra and panties, she stepped under the warm spray, languishing in the wonderful feel of it cascading down over her shoulders and back.

As much as Tallie would have liked to prolong this moment, she didn't intend to outstay her welcome. She washed, lathered then rinsed her hair, and turned off the water. Stepping out of the shower, she quickly dried herself. She hated putting on the same dirty clothes, and still wasn't convinced the spider had vacated her pants. Could she borrow one of Cole's tees?

She pulled a navy blue T-shirt from the drawer and quickly pulled it on over her head. It reached to her knees. Feeling adequately covered, she gathered her dirty clothes into a bundle, hung the towel to dry, combed her hair and went downstairs to the den.

Settling on the oversize sofa, she closed her eyes and tried to relax. It was then the nausea hit, hard and fast. She ran back up the stairs and into the bathroom she'd just used, not stopping until she was standing in front of the toilet. She hated the daily sickness. Hopefully when she went into her second trimester it would stop. She thought back to how Dr. Sterling had tried to talk her out of coming here, concerned about her safety. But Tallie wouldn't break the promise she'd made to her grandmother. She reasoned that wherever she was, she would still be sick.

The bout of sickness over, she rinsed her mouth then took a cooling sip of water. Better. She grabbed a new toothbrush from inside the cabinet and brushed her teeth, hoping it was over for the day.

She couldn't blame anyone but herself for her condition. When you got tipsy in New Orleans and were approached by the man of your dreams, this was what could happen. And in her case, it had happened. But even when the doctor had confirmed her condition, she'd still had a tough time grasping it. A baby. A tiny new soul.

The one thing that still angered her was how the

man had just disappeared before the sun rose the next morning, not giving her a chance to learn his identity. Just who in the hell did he think he was to degrade her in such a manner?

Cole was waiting for her when she returned to the den.

"Can I get a ride back from you?"

He stood staring at her for the longest time. "Are you ill?"

She shrugged and prayed he couldn't see the blush that crossed her face. "Just a bug I picked up somewhere. It's better now."

"Are you sure you don't want to stay here? We have plenty of room."

"Thank you, but I would prefer to return to the little cabin. I can walk if you don't have the time."

"Walk? Through a mile of trees and wheat until you find another spider or stumble over a snake?" He shook his head at the idea. "If you insist on going, let's go."

With a small white bag holding her clothes, she followed Cole out to his truck.

"You do know that attempting to live in that old shack puts you in every kind of danger. Why don't you just pack it in for now and come back in the fall when the weather is cooler and there are a lot fewer bugs? The camping conditions will be better."

In the fall Tallie would be caring for her new-born baby.

"I'm afraid I have other commitments then," she said. "Besides, by then I won't have access to the area. We both know as soon as I leave construction will commence."

He didn't argue with her. Masters just wanted her gone and apparently he would say or do anything to achieve it.

The next morning she had just finished dressing when she heard the sound of men's voices coming from the direction of the dig site. She stepped outside onto the cabin's porch and, sure enough, there were three men with shovels standing around the dig. She pulled on her boots and headed in their direction. Before she could close the distance, the men put their shovels to good use.

She broke into a jog. As she grew closer she saw where they had already churned her carefully laid out site in three different directions.

"Stop! Please stop!" she called out as she got to the men, who immediately halted their digging. "What are you doing? Who are you?"

One of the men removed his hat. "We work for the Circle M Ranch. Cole sent us up here to help you out. He said take some shovels and dig at the spot you had marked out."

"If you aren't careful, you might destroy something that's hundreds if not thousands of years old. What I'm looking for…it's very old and fragile."

The man who'd spoken looked at the other two and they all shrugged. "We're just doing what we were told to do, ma'am."

"And unless we hear differently from our boss, we have to keep digging," the second man chimed in.

"That's ridiculous." She faced the third man, who appeared to be the oldest of the three. "I'll go and speak with Mr. Masters. Until this is straightened out, please stop digging."

The first man put his cowboy hat back on and looked at the other two. "I'm not sure Cole is here. He was going to fly into Dallas. You may have missed him. But we'll wait an hour or so to give you a chance to talk with him. After that, we pretty much have to follow his orders."

She turned and hurried up the hill to her Ford wagon. She would tell Masters exactly what he could do with his orders. Normally a careful driver, she slammed her foot down on the accelerator and the old vehicle fishtailed several times before she reached the paved road leading to the mansion on the hill. How could he do this?

When she reached the parking area she hopped from her old Ford car and jogged toward the mansion.

After several frantic rings of the bell, a housekeeper answered the door. "I'm sorry," she said. "Mr. Masters just left. He's headed for the airstrip some distance behind the barn. Don't know if you can catch him, but it's that way if you want to try." She pointed toward the large barn and stables.

With quick thanks thrown over her shoulder, Tallie got back in her vehicle and headed out of the parking area. Following the directions, she almost immediately spotted the private air strip and the giant warehouse that housed the planes. There appeared to be only one thing in motion: a helicopter on the far left of the airfield with MASTERS CORPORATION on the side. As she got closer she could see Cole at the controls. He was writing something on a notepad and hadn't seen her approach. Tallie pulled up close to the helipad just as the rotor blade increased its speed. Knowing what was at stake, she leaped from her wagon car, ran to the chopper and pulled open the door.

The look on Cole's face was a mix of surprise, frustration and anger. Tallie silently glared at him. If looks could kill, he'd be a dead man. With obvious reservations he shut off the motor and the blades slowed. Pulling off the headset, he tossed it on the seat next to him and got out of the chopper. He was not happy. But neither was she.

"What in the hell do you think you're doing?" he bellowed as he reached her side of the helicopter.

"I might ask you the same question."

"You could have been killed."

"So what would you care?" Tallie was so furious her hands were held in tightly formed fists at her sides. "You send three of your ranch hands to my dig to destroy it. Then you sneak out so I can't contact you. You've reached a new low, Masters."

"I was trying to offer you some help," he argued. "And I've never *snuck* away from anything."

She could tell that her accusation had hit the target. She had him on the defensive, which was good.

"I've already told you it takes time and patience to extract the soil. You chop up a five-thousand-year-old artifact and it's game over. If that happens, this would all be for nothing. My time here meaningless. And the delay to your project pointless, as well."

"It appears to me that's already the case."

"You just don't get it. Is it that you don't want to understand or are you incapable of understanding?"

"Dr. Finley—"

"You did this on purpose. You might have destroyed an invaluable historical object. You didn't even tell your employees what they were doing. Just to dig. I hope you aren't that sloppy directing your companies."

That appeared to hit the nail squarely on the head. His eyes narrowed while his jaw muscles worked overtime; no doubt he was biting his tongue.

"So, what do you want, Dr. Finley? I'm late for a meeting in Dallas."

She coughed out a sarcastic laugh. "You have to ask? You have three cowboys with shovels digging up my site. Figure it out. Tell them to stop. Tell them to go away. Would you like for me to write it down for you? Do I need to lead you by the hand? Tell them to go mend a fence or shoe a horse or something."

Cole shook his head, not bothering to try to hide his frustration. "Fine. If you will kindly step back from the aircraft, I'll tell them to stop digging."

"I'll be watching."

"I'm sure you will." The sarcasm was heavy in

his tone. She didn't care. Not knowing if she could trust him after this stunt, she returned to the wagon and backed away from the helipad but waited to see which direction he would go. Within minutes the chopper lifted off and made a beeline for the dig site where it made a perfect landing. Cole was talking to the men as she pulled up next to the old shack.

He saw her and walked to the helicopter before she could get there. It lifted off and headed south toward Dallas, the rotors slapping the air like thunder in the sky. The men were already putting their shovels and other tools back in their truck. "Ma'am," the older cowboy said and nodded before he turned and walked to their pickup. Soon Tallie was left alone with only the birds to keep her company.

She didn't believe for a second that Cole had done this to help her. He'd thought he could sabotage her into leaving. He could think again. He had started a war and made it worse by making her miss her morning tea, and that was an unforgivable offense. She picked up her shovel and began the daunting task of checking for any destruction and ensuring no artifacts were embedded in the churned soil.

After many hours, she was convinced she'd been lucky. She emptied shovelful after shovelful into the sifter. There were arrowheads, broken pieces of pottery, a few beads made within the past few hundred years and not evidence of the lost tribe she was looking for, which was much older. The digging didn't seem to have caused any damage, though. She logged each one, took a picture and noted the day and time and other facts about each piece in her journal. She might be wrong about the date of the pieces but she didn't think so.

The sun was setting behind the far hills when the last sifting was completed. She would have to wait until the morning to outline a new grid. Trudging back to the cabin she fell onto the rickety old bed and kicked off her boots. Exhaustion propelled her to sleep with one last thought: what would Cole Masters try to pull tomorrow?

Five

It was a feeling rather than a sound that woke Tallie from a deep sleep. Her eyes opened just enough that she could tell it was before dawn. She felt eyes on her. Slowly sitting up, she looked out the door opening. A cow was standing in the doorway. Before she could pull on some jeans, another cow poked his head in over the first. Then a third came in low, as if to see what the other two had found.

"Shoo!" she screeched, stomping her foot at the heifers in the doorway. Her actions had no effect.

She swung a piece of cardboard at them and finally they took the hint and moved back. How many cows were there? Ten—at least—standing around the old shack. Slipping on her jeans and boots, she readied for war. Reaching back to her bedroll, she grabbed the white sheet from inside. Waving it and shouting "shoo" and "get out" finally caused a reaction. The entire group headed away from the cabin toward a fence with a wire gate half off its hinges. The cows kept going. When all were through the partial opening, Tallie quickly closed the gate. She hoped they weren't hurt by the wire but dreaded to see the damage they had caused to her camp and the dig site.

An hour later she was still picking up pieces of garbage from the bright blue barrels that had been overturned on the porch. She didn't know how much time it took to clean up all the mess. Only one thing she knew for sure: this was Cole Masters's doing. He was behind it. She couldn't prove it, but she knew it all the same.

She was sitting on the ramshackle porch still rolling up the last of the orange twine when she heard a pickup come down the path.

"Good morning, Dr. Finley," Cole said as he exited the truck.

She glared at him. If she opened her mouth she would chew him up and spit him out.

"So, how is your day?"

She shrugged.

"I don't know if you saw them, but about a dozen heifers with cuts and scratches showed up at the barn. Looks like they were run through a fence. I don't suppose you would know anything about that?"

She shrugged again. "Can't say I do. I've been

right here, on the property, all morning. No cows are allowed in this area, isn't that what you told me?"

His jaw worked overtime. He'd been caught in a trap of his own making.

"Yeah." He stared, suspicion marring his handsome features. "That's what I said."

"If I see a cow within the borders of the dig site, I'll be sure to let you know."

"You do that." He sounded skeptical. "What happened to your string?"

She shrugged her shoulders. "Part of it unraveled." She stated the obvious. Of course, it had had a bit of help. "Are you on some sort of leave? I mean I haven't seen you go to work but a couple of times since I've been here."

"You think I need to go to Dallas and work?"

"Well, Dallas or New York…wherever you have offices." She shrugged again. "It just seems odd to me that you're spending so much time out here worrying about cows and directing your ranch hands to 'help' me. That can't be very profitable."

She set the roll of string aside, leaned back against one of the posts supporting the roof over the porch and looked at him.

"I originally intended to use this period to oversee the initial phase of construction on my project and, as you know, that has been…postponed. So now I have free time to check on you and your progress. I see you sitting back rolling up a ball of string and I get curious. Shouldn't you be grabbing your little rake and brushing at dirt?"

Tallie's nostrils flared in anger. She wasn't a violent person, but in her mind's eye she could see her hand popping him on the back of his head for all of his lamebrained failed attempts to make her leave. "All in good time. It sounds like you're preoccupied with shutting me down." She looked at him and forced a smile. "I wouldn't go to too much trouble. I'm pretty stubborn as well as resilient."

He muttered something she couldn't understand before turning and walking toward his truck. And Tallie patted herself on the back for winning another round with the stubborn billionaire.

The days stretched into weeks and Tallie still hadn't found any proof of an ancient tribe. She was frustrated and tired of being sick. Every day. The morning sickness visited her in the afternoon now.

One morning during her fifth week on site, Tallie stretched and yawned as the sun rose over the distant hills. The past month had reminded her of both the positive and negative aspects of being on a dig. She felt soreness in her entire body. Concern for the baby made her slow down and take short breaks more often. Even if she ran out of time and found nothing, her *ipokini* would have understood.

Grabbing a stick leaning against the base of the old wood-burning stove, she clanged it against the metal and yawned again. By the fourth ding, the two skunks waddled out from under the bed and headed for the front door.

"You guys need to find a day job."

Normally she wouldn't allow houseguests but she'd been so tired the past few days, she just came inside after her bath in the river and dropped. If they didn't bother her or bite her toes, she would pay them the same courtesy. Her food was locked up in the Ford so there was nothing in the cabin to entice them. She figured they rummaged all night in places unknown and joined her in the shack just before daylight. Where they went now was anyone's guess.

She had just finished her morning tea when the sound of an engine—or engines—shredded the air. Stepping out onto the porch, she was shocked to see about a dozen four-wheelers top the rise near the cabin and continue on, making a large loop that took in the hills and valleys…and her current dig site. They didn't ride over the string that clearly defined the current grid but came close to it. A man in a pickup rode behind them, stopping on occasion to post a numbered sign.

What had Masters done now? With her mouth drawn into a straight line, she set her teacup down on the porch and angrily walked in that direction.

"Excuse me," she said, dodging two more riders as they topped the hill. "What is this?"

"Good morning, ma'am," the man replied, tipping his hat. "This is the day we have our Wheels for Wishing charity event. There are various skill levels and, by the end of the day, the rider with the fastest time will win the trophy and the grand prize. Of course, all the money including the grand prize will go to the charity. This year it's for the orphanage in Calico Springs. The owners of the Circle M Ranch always let us hold it on their land. Different locations each year, so no one has an advantage over the new contestants."

"And this year it's here."

"Yes, ma'am." He nodded. "But don't you worry. Cole told us you were working in the area and cautioned us to be sure to stay clear of your archeology site."

"Oh, he did?"

"We drew out the course together, just to be sure."

A calm seemed to come over her. She had to give Masters kudos for his determination. This time, however, she wasn't going to lose her temper. She was not going to ask him what he thought he was doing. He knew full well what he was doing. And she had no intention of leaving. No, this time she was going to give him a taste of his own medicine.

"Where is Mr. Masters?"

"He had business in Dallas, but he'll be back late this afternoon."

That should be just about right.

The people at the copy store in town were more than willing to lend assistance, helping her to put on paper an eye-catching announcement. Buzzy and his friends who, excited at getting five dollars for their efforts, began to spread the several hundred flyers all around the small town.

The ground below was carpeted in every size, make and model of vehicle produced in the past twenty years. It was a virtual smorgasbord of metal roofs and hood tops in every color under the sun. It would be an amazing sight to behold if it hadn't been on the grounds surrounding his house. Cole flew in close, making a small circle above the cars and trucks, curious what in the hell these people were doing.

It looked like they were making toasts: people were coming and going in and out of the house holding glasses up toward him. Those who swarmed the swimming pool clapped. And he could hear what sounded like rock-and-roll music above the sound of the helicopter's engine. In the far distance there were more parked cars surrounding the circular route chosen for the four-wheeler competition.

Cole quickly landed the chopper and stormed toward the house. His cell in his hand, he tried to contact his security team. The phone was finally answered with, "Hey, Mr. M. You're just in time. The second round of pizzas was just delivered."

"Is this Marco? Meet me in my office in two minutes." He ended the call.

As Cole made it through the back lawn and pool area, he was greeted with shouts of "Thank you" and a drink was pushed into his hand—perfect timing. The crowd parted, opening a path to his back door. Before he ever got to his office he'd ascertained what was happening and knew without any doubt whatsoever a certain archeologist was to thank for all her trouble.

After meeting with his security detail, he strolled

outside, letting his eyes search the crowds around the pool. He spotted several ranch hands and more than half the residents of the town and, in the middle of it all, there she was. Miss Let's-Throw-a-Party, kicked back in a lounger wearing the tiniest hot-pink string bikini he'd ever seen in his life. How did one approach such a sight and keep his anger in the foreground?

"Dr. Finley," he said, his hands on his hips. "Great party you're hosting."

She looked up over the sunglasses perched on her nose. "Oh, it isn't my party. It was a work day until the four-wheeler festivities began." She laid back and pushed her glasses farther up her nose. "What's the old saying…if you can't beat 'em, join 'em?"

About then someone did a belly flop into the pool, sending a wave of water directly toward Cole's backside.

"Hey, see if you can find a chair and enjoy the perfect weather."

His jaw muscles worked convulsively. *If you can't beat 'em…* He looked around and spotted an empty lounger. Within a few seconds he had dragged the chair next to Tallie and sprawled out beside her. If his action surprised her she hid it well.

"You're gonna get too hot in those clothes."

"How nice of you to notice. Maybe you would like to help me take them off?"

"So glad you could make it for the celebration," she said, ignoring his question.

"Actually the party is over. The security detail

will be making the rounds shortly. I couldn't pass up the opportunity to share a couple of moments with a gorgeous woman."

She tensed. "Why do men see only the outside?"

"Because we're men." He looked over at her. "That's just what we do. But...give us the chance to get to know a woman and it's amazing how fast the old heart can start tripping all over itself."

"You talk as if you know that from experience."

He nodded. "Maybe I do. Have dinner with me tonight, Tallie. You've lost the entire day, might as well waste the evening, too."

She turned and stared at him. "You want me to have dinner with you?"

"Absolutely." He sat up from the recliner. "Unlike some among us, I don't hold grudges."

"Can't say I know what you're talking about, but I have to work tonight. Catch up the discovery log. And I don't really want to get into another...*discussion* of why I can't just leave now."

"But here's something you might keep in mind. I can make a large contribution to the museum if certain needs are met."

"And what would those needs be?"

"Postpone your dig."

"Not happening."

"You're sure about dinner?"

"I'm sure, and here's why. You are a spoiled egomaniac who thinks he's a hotshot. But you want to kick back, lose the bad boy, hottest-man-of-the-year reputation and be a real guy for a change. And my weakness is falling for guys like you. My strength is saying no to them. Now, if you'll excuse me."

Cole reflected on the irony of what she'd just said. Tallie *had* fallen for him, in a big way, in New Orleans. It was a small miracle that she still didn't recognize him—or was that just an act? He needed to figure out what she was up to.

She stood from her chair and smiled. That perfect little grin that made him crazy. He would remember this. He hadn't been played this well in...maybe forever. Still, paybacks for Dr. Finley would be priceless. She wouldn't get away with this.

But why did that little voice of reason in the back of his mind keep repeating, *Yeah, she will*...

Tallie swung her feet to the floor and got out of bed. She had a long day ahead of her. She quickly got dressed, grabbed the bottled water and headed to the wagon to get her tea. But the can was empty. She dug down inside the boxes of rations. No tea. In fact, she realized she was out of almost everything.

In the past few days, she'd made real progress on the site. She had just begun to find tiny pieces of pottery she was almost certain came from the 1500s or earlier. She hated to interrupt her work now. But she'd learned long ago, no tea, no clear head. No clear head, no work. So, to the store she would go.

The small town of Calico Springs was only about ten miles from the dig site. Returning to civilization always felt good but odd. It didn't take her long to find what she needed, including her tea. To be safe, she grabbed two more cans. She added a can of insect repellent that hopefully was better than the first she'd bought and a box of mothballs to the items in her cart. Somebody had long ago told her skunks wouldn't tread over mothballs. She didn't have anything to lose.

Once she'd purchased the supplies, it was back to the dig site. On the way she called in to Dr. Sterling at the museum. He was excited about the slivers of pottery she'd found in the past few days. He encouraged her to keep at it as long as her condition would allow, apologizing again for not having enough staff to send someone to help her.

The remaining seven weeks would go fast and, before she knew it, she would be out of time. That was one thing her boss didn't need to remind her of. She had Cole Masters for that.

Only a mile from the cabin the car began to pull hard to the left. *Crud. Not a flat. Please.* But when she got out and checked, that was exactly what she had. She looked around at the same rolling hills she'd been gazing at since the day she'd arrived. No human in sight.

Tallie walked to the back of the vehicle and began taking boxes of groceries out to get to the spare tire. The spare tire rack had long since stopped functioning so the tire had to be stored in the back along with everything else. She crossed her fingers the jack was with it and the spare had some air.

She was in luck. She found the jack and when she bounced the spare out of the vehicle she was pleased to see that it had plenty of air. But then she popped off the hubcap only to find the lug nuts were rusted onto the bolts. She stood, arched her back and considered her alternatives. It would take a dozen trips to carry her supplies to the camp. She might have phone service but no clue whom to call. It looked like this would cost her a full day of digging.

She heard a pickup coming down the private road, turned and saw Cole Masters behind the wheel. Of all the possible white knights, why did it have to be him? She didn't want to be indebted to this surly man for anything.

He pulled up next to her and got out of his truck.

"Give me the lug wrench."

"I can do this myself. Thanks anyway."

"There might be a spider lurking behind the tire."

She glared. "It must be nice not to fear anything."

He snatched the tool out of her hand, lowered the car until the wheel was firmly back on the ground and loosened the rusty bolts in less time than it would have taken her to remove one brand-new one. As she watched him work, she was again struck with the feeling that she'd met him before. Something about him seemed familiar. It was then that she saw it: a small tattoo, partially revealed in the vee of his shirt collar where it was unbuttoned.

"You have a tattoo," she ventured. "What is it, if you don't mind me asking?"

He froze. Then he turned the last lug nut, pulled off the tire and stood. "You've probably seen one like it at some point." He pulled aside the collar on the shirt.

"That's cool. You know I do remember seeing one like it." She frowned with a shrug. "I just can't remember where."

He merely smiled. It was a humorless smile that only amplified the little warning bells going off in her head. What was he up to now?

Today he was wearing black jeans and a black shirt. His hair had grown out since she'd first arrived at the ranch and it looked shaggy and wind-blown. If you took away his beard, he'd look exactly the way the stranger had looked that night in New Orleans.

She stepped back from him, her heart thundering in her chest and her eyes growing wide. It couldn't be. It. Could. Not. Be. Was Cole Masters the man she'd...*met*...in New Orleans? She shook her head in denial. It was impossible. The man who had taken her to bed was nice. He wasn't arrogant. There might be an uncanny resemblance, but the two men were completely different.

But everything fit; all the pieces suddenly slammed together. Cole would be the kind of guy to have treated her the way he had. He probably either borrowed the clothes he'd worn or visited a thrift store. *So no one would recognize him.* He didn't live under a bridge or in a run-down apartment in New Orleans. He lived in multiple mansions around the world. She recalled a couple of news articles she'd read after Dr. Sterling had warned her to be wary of Cole Masters.

Dr. Sterling had no idea just how right that warning had been.

Six

She took a step back as the truth washed over her. "You knew. All this time. You knew and you didn't bother to tell me?"

"I was curious how long it would take you."

Her emotions were all over the place. She pressed her hands against her forehead. She could feel the blood surging to her head while her heart pounded in her chest.

"You are an arrogant, sneaky, sabotaging, lying, two-faced billionaire." She turned to march back to her truck. "Is this how you get your kicks? You... you play with people's emotions?"

In her mind a war raged. Was this the same guy she had met and shared a bed with or was he trying to mess with her? The man she'd met in New Orleans might have been a derelict but he was a nice derelict. She could feel the blush run up her neck and across her face. Even the tips of her ears felt hot.

Her mind was whirling. She couldn't stop staring at Cole as she desperately tried to dispel the notion that he was the sexy stranger who had so easily and proficiently taken her to bed. A stranger. One who did magic things with his hands, his mouth, his body. The memory of that night would stay with her forever.

"You lied to me."

"No, I didn't."

"Yes, you did. If you'd been honest, you would have told me as soon as you knew I didn't recognize you. And I wouldn't have recognized you without the tattoo. And the dark shirt. And the jeans."

What was he grinning about?

"I've never done that before, just so you know," she added.

"Done what?"

"Gone to bed with a complete stranger."

"It was a great night. Why are you apologizing?"

"I'm not apologizing," she retorted. "I just wanted to set the record straight."

"It doesn't matter."

"It matters to *me*."

He stood and rubbed his hands together. "I didn't do anything you didn't want me to do. You worry too much. We both had a great time. That's all that counts. It just isn't a big deal."

The more he shrugged it off, the angrier she got.

"So picking up a stranger in a bar is the norm for you? How very sad."

"No." He rested his hands on his waist and held her gaze. "As a matter of fact, that was a first for me, as well. But I can't say I'm sorry."

"I wouldn't be so sure about that."

He frowned, obviously not understanding.

"You left me there," she continued. "You left me to wake up alone without even knowing your name. Who does that?"

"Look, Tallie—"

"No. Don't 'look, Tallie' me. What if you had a disease? For that matter, what if I had a disease?"

"I took precautions. Anyway, we both know it's all right now."

Oh, how she wanted to tell him how it wasn't all right. Before she could gather the words Cole spoke.

"Tallie, I admit I could have handled it better. But everywhere I go, at least several times a month, I come in contact with a woman or a tight little group who sends in a woman to try and entrap me. If we have sex, a false pregnancy claim will shortly follow. If we arrive at a restaurant, you can set your watch by how soon she will accidently fall. Or step in a hole walking up to my front door and sprain her ankle so that she can sue. In New Orleans, when I told you I wasn't into a long or permanent relationship, I meant it. If I recall, you said the same thing. I'm not a family man. I never will be. I don't want a wife and I don't want kids. For all I knew, you could have been like any of those other women. I never thought I would see you again, so why bother with formalities?"

He tossed the tire iron in the back of her vehicle and walked toward her.

"You could have asked me my name. I know my own name and I wouldn't mind sharing it. Especially...especially under the circumstances."

"At the time I wasn't thinking. I don't think you were, either."

She couldn't argue with that. She was still trying to swallow the fact that Cole was her dream man. And it had nothing to do with money. Their coming together in New Orleans was like something out of a movie or a romantic novel. At least it had been until she'd confirmed she was pregnant.

But now she had her answer. If she told him she was carrying his child he would accuse her of all sorts of awful things. Tears welled in her eyes at the complete finality of the situation. Any dream that he would believe her and maybe even ask her to marry him was gone. She would raise the baby herself. She now knew without any shadow of doubt that was what she must do. He'd made it clear he wasn't a family man. He wanted no kids.

Considering how unconcerned he was about their time together in New Orleans, he wouldn't care two hoots about a baby. Or he would accuse Tallie of getting pregnant on purpose. She could think of a half dozen scenarios and none of them was pleasant. Tallie refused to bring a child into this world and subject him to a father who was never going to show up. Every child deserved better. Hopefully, someday she would find a good man who would raise her baby as his own and Cole would never be the wiser. And her baby would not lack for anything in spite of the fact that she had no money to speak of. Love was more important than money. As long as she could provide a roof over their heads and food on the table, they would be fine.

In minutes, Cole had replaced the flat tire with the spare. He handed her the jack and tossed the flat into the back of his truck.

Tallie tried to maintain a grip on her emotions. She inhaled deeply to clear her mind of what she'd just learned. Better save it for later; she could work through all this devastating information when she was alone.

"I think the tire is fixable. I'll take it to the local garage and have it repaired."

"Thank you, Mr. Masters. I am in your debt," she choked out. He looked at her as though he just now realized her words said one thing but her body language said quite another.

"I think we're past the 'mister.' My name is Cole."

"I don't care what your name is, *Mr.* Masters. If I wasn't worthy of knowing it three months ago, I don't want to know it now."

"Tallie, you're being stubborn."

For the briefest of seconds she struggled with his comment. She did not want to be on a first-name basis with this man. He was not the same man she'd met in New Orleans, although she had to admit his current attitude matched the first glimpse she'd had of him: dark and ruthless. Dangerous. Being on a first-name basis was the first step to a relationship. She didn't want a relationship that had nowhere to go. It wasn't on her bucket list.

But neither was bearing his child.

Why did she have such bad luck with men? Her last relationship was a case in point. John Mosby, a guy she'd dated for a year, had been an egocentric control freak. She'd done everything he'd asked her to do and still he'd dumped her, sneaking his stuff out of her apartment while she was away on a dig. It hurt. Eventually she'd decided it was the best thing that could have happened to her. Like she'd had a choice. He hadn't even bothered to leave a note. She'd had the humiliating task of asking her girlfriends if they'd known what had happened to John.

But at least she was free of his constant, overbearing, fault-finding harassment. She wasn't about to jump from that frying pan into the Cole Masters's fire.

"Go ahead and I'll follow you to your camp site just to be sure nothing else happens."

"No."

She turned to go back to her vehicle when he seized her shoulders and spun her around. She opened her mouth to ask what he thought he was doing and his lips came down over hers. For seconds she struggled, but his lips, the taste of him, were potent, overcoming her stubborn resolve to not make another mistake with this man. As soon as she relented he kissed her long and deep, and moments later raised his head, leaving her lips swollen. Leaving her wanting more.

"I want to start fresh, learn more about you other than how insanely phenomenal you are in bed." His deep voice was raspy. Her body immediately responded.

He lowered his head, his lips almost touching hers. "Could we start over, Tallie?" Then he was kissing her again, and this time she felt his hunger and it drew her to him. His tongue moistened her lips before plunging deep inside the cavern of her mouth. She felt his hand at the back of her head, holding her to him as he continued to blow her mind. She heard him groan then he was backing away, making the heat of the day drop to below freezing.

She wanted his arms around her. She wanted him to kiss her some more, to make love to her. She was putty in his arms, encircled by the scent and strength and touch of him. She'd often dreamed of the night they had spent together, burning the sheets and making love until most sane people would have been satisfied. Not them. Every climax he'd given her would satisfy her for a while then he would say something to her in that remarkable voice or kiss her and nibble her jawline or find her breast with his hand and lips and she would be lost again.

But he was Cole Masters. *The* Cole Masters. Playboy of the western world. He knew what he was doing. He knew a woman's body as well as his own, so under the circumstances she couldn't agree to starting over. Eventually he would feel her enlarging belly and he would know. Then his professed interest would change into loathing because he would think she'd set him up; that she had gotten pregnant on purpose.

"I suppose we could talk." That was the most she was willing to do.

"If that's all you can give me right now, I'll take it. Maybe I can convince you otherwise. Go ahead and get in your car. I'll follow you to the cabin."

She got into her wagon, started the engine and looked in her rearview mirror. She had to grudgingly admit it had been nice of him to stop and help her change the tire. She had no experience with millionaires, let alone billionaires, but she doubted if anyone else of his social status would do what he'd done, especially after all the times they'd butted heads over the past several weeks.

After a twenty-minute drive, she pulled up next to the shack. By the time she got out of the truck Cole was already opening the back door to her wagon, asking where she wanted things to go.

"Okay, that's everything," Cole said as he closed the doors to her vehicle.

"I appreciate all you've done. I really—"

Cole pushed her against the side of his truck and, in the glow of the setting sun, kissed her again.

Tallie tried to push out of his arms but Cole was determined. It didn't take very many seconds until she was kissing him back. Her belly tightened as the heat ran rampant through her veins.

His hands moved to cup her face, holding her to him and sending sparks of pleasure along her spine. Finally she placed her smaller hands over his and he allowed her to push him back.

"Cole." She was breathing hard. Her lips were inches away from his, moist, swollen from his kisses, slightly open, wanting more. His member was rock-hard, just like before. And there would be no relief for either of them until he took her to his bed.

"Tallie, are you involved with anyone?"

Was it any of his business? "No."

Then he was kissing her again with an intensity that proclaimed his ownership. He pressed his erection against her and growled his claim.

She felt the intense heat from his body and fought the urge to slide her arms up over his shoulders and pull him closer to her. As she turned away, her breasts brushed against the hard contours of his chest. Her nipples jumped to full attention, sending an electrifying sensation through her entire body. She could sense the sexual charge between them when his body responded. She didn't move. She didn't have to. The awareness of her arousal was noted and returned.

"Tallie," he murmured as his mouth came down over her lips once again. The kiss was amazing, his lips soft and pliable yet firm at the same time. She wanted to melt into them. Into *him*. With a small whimper, she turned away but she'd had a reminder of just how seriously sexy, how potent, Cole Masters could be. It was enough to leave her wanting more. A lot more. She could sense his desire. They barely knew each other yet her body was throwing off hormones like fireworks on Independence Day. Fighting her own desire as well as his, she pushed out of his arms.

"I told you before, with the exception of our night in the French Quarter, I don't sleep around."

"Then why me?" he asked. "Why did you let me seduce you? Why was our night together different?" He looked at her long and hard before dropping his hands to his sides. It might be the first time in his life Cole Masters had been turned down.

"I suppose I drank too much. I lost track of who I really am."

"No. I think you found out who you really are. A beautiful, passionate woman who let her attraction to a man overcome her staid impractical beliefs."

With John it had taken months of knowing him to even get remotely close to the state Tallie was in right now if, in fact, she ever did. John had never cared enough to make the effort to turn her on. He was only in it to please himself.

But Cole didn't need to make any effort to turn her on. She felt her response to him loud and clear. His hard body was erect and ready. And all she had to do was say yes. The heat surged through her at the thought. But with determination she stepped back and this time he let her go.

She didn't know if he was trying to seduce her because he found something about her he liked, or if he was trying to seduce her into making her leave. It had to be one or the other. She had her doubts about the first possibility, though. In a lot of ways, she was still that gangly, naïve girl who had grasped hold of any attention John had offered and done what he'd wanted her to do because he was the only one who had ever showed any interest. So what would a man like Cole Masters see in her?

Then again, if he was trying to seduce her to have his way over the dig site, it could backfire on him. Seducing her, if she allowed it, would not make her leave any faster. In fact, it could very well further complicate the entire situation.

It was more than likely he saw her as weak and vulnerable. She had the education but she'd never experienced the level of sophistication he was used to. She'd never had a man of Cole's wealth and status coming on to her and she would be the first to admit she was completely out of her depth. He was probably taking advantage of any opportunity to talk her into abandoning the dig. He was a master manipulator who would warp any love session into forcing her to leave. She'd be stupid to discount that option; the most probable one under the circumstances.

"Good night, Cole." She turned and walked toward the front door of the shack. Stepping inside, she sat on the sleeping bag, absently watching as the lights from his truck shone through the holes in the sides and top of the cabin as he turned around then drove away.

She didn't know the man and he didn't know her. She didn't know how to get to know him without precariously dangling her heart on a string. If she were more worldly, she might say yes and see where it would go. But her experience with John painted a pretty clear and dismal picture of how men acted.

And she would never put herself in that situation again.

It was four o'clock in the afternoon the following day when the garage called about Tallie's tire. It couldn't be saved.

"Fine. Put a new one on my account." Cole started to end the call but thought better of it. "Ray? I need the new tire to look like the old one. Roll it in the mud a couple of times and walk your dog."

"Walk my dog?"

"Yeah. You know. *Walk your dog.* Let him do his business on the tire, then roll it in the dirt again."

"Cole, you ask for some strange things."

Cole couldn't help but laugh. "Thanks, Ray."

Clearly the man didn't understand the why of the request but he would do it. Cole suspected Tallie would insist on paying for the fix. She wouldn't be happy about an entirely new tire and he would have to listen to a long argument over a hundred bucks. No thanks. With any luck, he would accept her ten dollars for the "repaired" tire and that would be that.

By five o'clock the new tire was delivered. It looked pretty bad. Cole was impressed. He threw it in the back of his truck and headed for the dig site. *Damn.* She even had him calling it a dig site. Whatever, it was a good excuse to check on her progress, as if he needed one. She'd been working on the last section of her initial grid this morning. He couldn't help but wonder where she would go next.

He drove out to the site, pulled the new old tire out of the back of his truck and rolled it over to her vehicle. He was almost finished changing it out when she came around the corner.

"How much do I owe you?"

"Ten dollars."

"Ten dollars? For a new tire?" She gave him a look that clearly said nice try.

"I'll put it on the tab."

"Fine. I'll settle up before I leave."

And Cole believed she would. At least she would try.

Seven

It was not fully light the next morning when Tallie was awakened by an odd sound. It was as though someone had turned on a giant sprinkler. She looked toward the dig site. There was just enough light to see an irrigation system, silent and unused until now, watering the wheat. One of the sprayers appeared to be centered on the area she had planned on digging that day.

No way. This could not be happening. She quickly pulled on her jeans, a clean shirt and her boots, grabbed a sheet of plastic they used to preserve a site during a rain storm and hurried to the dig. Water was spewing at full throttle. She made an attempt to cover the ground where she'd planned to work. The soil had already become saturated.

She took a step forward and realized, belatedly, that her boots were stuck more than ankle deep in the reddish-brown mud. About then a blast of cold water hit her smack in the face, causing her to lose her balance. She fell to the left, her right foot sliding out of the boot. Turning onto her back, which seemed to be the only way to right herself, she sat up, struggling to pull her boots out of the now almost shin-deep mud. She succeeded in freeing one boot before another blast of water knocked her down again, this time face-first. At that point, a slow crawl was the only remaining option to escape.

Lumbering toward the end of the sprinkler, she attempted to turn it off. The thing was controlled remotely. As in, from the ranch. She didn't have to ask who'd done this.

As she sloshed back toward her Ford wagon, her anger grew with each step. It would be days before that area could be excavated. And the longer the sprinklers were on, the worse it would get. Cole Masters was behind this. The man just would not give up, but she had to admit after this stunt he was getting closer to inspiring her to pack her bags. Reaching the vehicle she started the engine and headed to Cole's ranch house.

She passed the Circle M Ranch sign over the entrance to the driveway. The blacktop road continued on, rising at a steady elevation until she arrived at the house. She got out of her Ford and followed the flagstone path up to the door. She rang the bell then knocked.

She would give him thirty seconds before she walked in. Her blood pressure was sending off warning signals, her ears were ringing and she prayed the horrible man would get to the door before she stroked out. There were few times over the course of her life she'd ever been this furious.

Just seconds before she reached for the knob, the door opened. Cole took one look, his eyes growing big at the sight of her. She knew what she must look like, wet and covered in dark red mud head to toe, with one boot on and the other still stuck in the mud back at camp. She glared at the preposterous man and then noticed another man rise from the sofa in the den behind him and slowly walk toward the open door where she stood.

"If you think, for one second, your little schemes will drive me away, you'd better think again." Her voice was quivering in anger. "Shut that irrigation system off. Now."

"Irrigation? The irrigation system is not scheduled to come on in that area. The wheat is about to be harvested. Because of both your dig and my project I had it shut down."

"Convince me."

"Tallie, I didn't do this." Cole held up his hands, palms forward in a gesture of surrender. But he pursed his lips as he tried to hide a grin. "I don't know what happened but I'll take care of it." He paused, allowing his eyes to roam over her from head to foot as if he couldn't believe what he'd seen the first time.

"You have fifteen seconds." She pinned him to the spot with her eyes, her finger poking at his chest. "This little gimmick will set me back days, but I'm not leaving. I refuse. You cannot run me off, Masters. Believe it. Deal with it."

"Come inside. Please."

She stepped inside, hoping to leave as much mud as possible. She nodded to the other man. He nodded back and also pursed his lips as though fighting not to laugh. "I'm Cole's brother, Wade. And you must be Dr. Finley."

"I would shake but…" She held out her mud-covered hand.

Cole reached for the phone and hit a speed dial number. "Yeah. Griff? I thought I instructed your boys to kill the watering on the east part of the forty thousand acres for a while." He listened quietly. "Well, whatever you did, it didn't work. The irrigation is going full-blast and has apparently destroyed Dr. Finley's excavation site. Shut it down now then find out who turned it on or fix what's wrong and call me when you make a determination." He ended the call.

"I'm sorry, Tallie, but I had nothing to do with this. Perhaps you can relocate to another area until that section of the site dries out. It would appear," he said as he once again let his eyes rake her from top to bottom, "that the site is too muddy to work."

"Ya think?" Fool that she was she believed him when he said he had no part in what happened, but he still had no appreciation for what she was trying to accomplish. "Do you even know or care what I'm trying to do out there?"

He shrugged. "Look for pieces of old pottery? I guess I really don't know. Should I?"

"No. No, you're right. It has nothing to do with you except to delay your project."

Shaking her head, she turned around and limped back outside to her vehicle. She had to go back and try to retrieve her other boot from the mud once the water was turned off. Pulling out her phone, she wiped the dried dirt from the screen and punched speed dial to the museum curator's private line.

"Tallie? Great to hear from you," Dr. Sterling said. "How's it going?"

"Excuse me, sir," said one of the house staff. "You are wanted on line one."

"Take a message."

"I'm afraid he's rather insistent. It's Governor Mitchell."

Cole snatched up the phone. "Governor?"

The man sounded angry. Cole caught two words: "attack" and "hose."

"What?"

The governor repeated himself.

"I most assuredly did not attack her with a water hose!"

"This is getting too good," Wade muttered from the sofa in Cole's home office.

Cole sat forward in his desk chair. "It was a problem with the irrigation system and it's being repaired as we speak."

"I shouldn't have to tell you that Dr. Finley is there on a very important assignment. I would expect you to assist her in any way you can. From what I was told, you also tried to sabotage her dig in other ways." Governor Mitchell paused. "Cole, I've known you boys for a lot of years and, frankly, I'm surprised and disheartened by the reports I'm getting from the director of the museum where Dr. Finley works."

Cole was seething. He found himself out of his chair and pacing around his office. *She* did this. Governor Mitchell had been a family friend for most of his lifetime. But apparently Cole wasn't the only one in the picture who carried some weight. And right now Tallie's side was winning.

"It was all a misunderstanding, Ted," Cole said in what he hoped was a convincing tone. "I was attempting to lend assistance not destroy her work."

"I'd have to say your assistance blew up in your face," the governor replied. "As I understand, she only has another six or seven weeks. Try and work with this woman, Cole. She's highly regarded in the academic community. Graduated with the highest honors and is well on her way to becoming one of the top researchers in her field. It would not bode well for either of us if she botched this dig and you were the reason behind it."

"I understand."

"I hope you do," he returned. "So, how are

Chance and Holly? Is married life treating them well?" Cole's younger brother, Chance, had just gotten married a little over a year ago.

"Yes. They're doing great." A lot better than he was. "They just moved into their own house here on the ranch. It's kind of you to ask."

"You tell them both I sent my regards. To Wade, too," the governor said.

"I certainly will, Governor. Thanks for your call."

Cole hung up the phone and felt the room spinning around him. He looked at Wade, who sat five feet away still trying not to laugh. "Governor Mitchell sends his regards."

"I take it that call was about our little archeologist?"

"Don't say a word," Cole warned his brother.

"The two of you make a cute couple."

"Wade, I'm warning you."

"When did you meet her?"

"What does it matter?"

"Exactly."

"New Orleans. That weekend I stayed over after the Coleman merger."

"New Orleans? Interesting."

"Shut up or leave."

"This just gets better and better."

"I think she's in cahoots with someone who doesn't want me to finish my project."

"Maybe if you offered to help her, she would complete her mission faster and get out of your way."

"Tried. Failed."

"What did Mitchell want?"

"The irrigation thing. Someone told him I attacked her with a garden hose," Cole said.

"And you would never do that."

"I didn't!" Cole's anger returned. "Okay, I did have Red and a couple of the boys go digging on her site."

"Bro, you are bad. What else?"

"I asked Stuart to turn some heifers loose in the pasture. She ran them right through the damned fence. Not only did I have to have somebody put up a new fence, Holly spent a week bandaging cuts and giving tetanus shots. But the damned sprinkler system wasn't me."

The most irritating part of the whole thing was that, despite everything, Cole still found her exceedingly attractive. He had even envisioned helping her clean the mud from her body, making certain to check every square inch. The thought had come to him while she'd stood there miserable and soaked to the skin, pointing her finger at him, and he still couldn't shake the image from his mind.

He wished they had met under different circumstances. But when he thought about it, they actually had. If only he could rewind to what they'd shared that weekend in New Orleans. He would have liked to get to know her and see where it would go from there. But with their current situation, it wasn't in the cards. She couldn't stand him for reasons that were obvious. And she made him crazy. He didn't exactly know how to get around that. He refused to grovel. So he would move on, suppress his feelings, and no one would be the wiser.

Eight

"Cole?"

It was Debra Davis, his secretary, a middle-aged woman who'd been his right hand for almost ten years. Hopefully she was calling him to give him the good news that something—a loophole, a favor, money—*something* had been found that would remove the good doctor from his land once and for all.

He knew he was on shaky ground. Tallie was just too damn tempting. In fact she was the first woman in all the years since Gina's death who'd touched him on a level he never thought he would feel again. He needed to keep his eye on the ball, to stay focused on building the corporate retreat. Every time he came in contact with Tallie he lost his mind. He wasn't getting much sleep. Had no appetite. And her beautiful face was always in his thoughts. It was all he could do to stay away. This last-ditch effort to remove her was as much for self-preservation as it was the project.

"Talk to me, Debra."

The silence on the other end of the line was not a good sign.

"There's nothing," his secretary finally said.

"What do you mean there's nothing?" Cole asked, sitting forward in his chair, ready for some serious explanations. Debra was the best. She could find information where there wasn't any. She could make things happen that seemed impossible. She was Cole's genius at the controls. No one could best Debra. This was not the answer he'd anticipated but after receiving the report from his security division, he wasn't surprised.

"I checked with Jeremy—" the lead counsel at Masters Corporation "—the court, Dr. Finley's boss at the museum. There's no way around it. Sorry, Cole, but it looks like you're stuck with her for fifty-one more days."

This was not happening. He'd dealt with bureaucratic red tape before but this was pure insanity.

"See if you can get him on the line, Debra."

"One moment." And it literally only took Cole's assistant one moment to get Tallie's boss on the phone.

"This is Henry Sterling."

"Dr. Sterling? Cole Masters. Thank you for taking my call."

"Of course, Mr. Masters. How can I help you?"

"As I'm sure you know, one of your archeologists, Dr. Finley, is working on some land I own in Calico County."

"Yes. We are all most excited about the possibility of what she may discover." He caught himself, apparently realizing that would not be why Cole was calling. "Your administrative assistant called earlier, asking if the dig could be postponed or cancelled. I'm afraid I couldn't accommodate her."

Cole had to make the man understand his need for Tallie to leave. "I don't know if you are aware but I am in the process of developing that land. In fact, I have cement trucks standing by to pour the foundations for both the main lodge and thirty cabins. Then a pool will be constructed along with other amenities. The dig, as she refers to it, is causing me a serious delay."

"That is regretful."

"It's more than regretful."

Cole felt his frustration rise to the surface. "I'm sitting around twiddling my thumbs while she scrutinizes dirt." Which wasn't entirely true. He had plenty of projects needing his attention, but this was *his* project. Other than the sheer indignity he would suffer if this venture fell apart, his brothers would never let him live it down, all in good-natured joking, but still… Plus, he needed Tallie off his land for a very personal reason. The longer he was presented with the temptation of this woman, the harder it was to keep a hold on his sanity. "Why is there no one helping her?"

"Unfortunately all of the archeologists and even the approved volunteers from both the museum and the university are tied up on other projects. Dr. Finley was scheduled to join a dig in Brazil that is also short on manpower as soon as she finishes at your property."

"Was?"

There was a long pause. "You understand I can't discuss Dr. Finley's employment or any health issues she might have. Let me just say that her participation in the Brazil dig is still to be determined."

"Of course." It struck Cole as odd that Dr. Sterling would bring up her health. What medical condition could she possibly have? He hoped it wasn't cancer or some equally horrific disease. His heart did a flip-flop in his chest. Guilt at giving her such a hard time almost overwhelmed him. "Why don't you hire more people? That would seem to be the obvious solution."

"Primarily the problem is a severely limited budget. We just don't have the resources to fulfill the needs of all the sites allotted to us. Pretty much par for course, unfortunately. Dr. Finley is donating her time and some of her own money to see her project finished. Perhaps you can—"

"So what if my corporation made a donation? Enough for you to hire, say, a dozen people for a year?"

"We are always delighted to receive donations,

but I must tell you that isn't the way it works here. Donations are handled through the museum's board of directors. They decide the allocation of funds. There are many other programs that are waiting for backing besides archeology-related projects."

When Cole made no response, Dr. Sterling added, "I am genuinely sorry for your inconvenience, Mr. Masters. If it's any consolation, Dr. Finley is one of our more highly educated specialists with dual degrees in both archeology and biological and forensic anthropology. I have no doubt she will work as hard as possible to complete the dig as soon as she can."

"Are you telling me there is no one I can call and offer to pay them to help her?"

"Not as far as I know. You might try calling the State Archeology Program Center. Perhaps they know something I don't. Would you like that number?"

This was insane. "I'll pass on the number. Thanks for your time." Cole ended the call.

Before he could stand, his private line rang. "Yes?"

"Cole, I forgot to remind you..." Debra sounded a bit hesitant. Again. What could it be this time?

"The ground-breaking ceremony for the retreat is next week. On Friday. I was afraid you might have forgotten under the circumstances."

He had indeed. "You'll have to cancel it."

Another hesitation. "I can't. The RSVPs have been confirmed with a card from you, thanking them for coming to this—"

"I know what the cards say," he snapped. *God damn.* Some twenty potential investors would be arriving on Thursday. And on Friday they would be escorted to the site where the main lodge would be constructed. Would they see a foundation? Oh, no. Hell, no. They would see one little red flag among two hundred other little red flags and a woman crawling around in the dirt in the middle of it all.

"The limos are set and ready to meet each flight, pick up the guest at the airport and escort them to the hotel then bring them to the project site." Debra stopped talking and the silence was deafening.

"Cole?"

"I'm here." But he sure as hell didn't want to be.

"Have you used your...skills?" He could picture Debra with that irritating smirk on her face. The one she used every time she caught him in some peculiar situation. He appreciated her humor and positive thinking. Except at times like this. "You can be pretty persuasive when you set your mind to it. *Dallas* magazine didn't name you Bachelor of the Year three times for nothing."

This nightmare just would not end. He wasn't about to confess to Debra that the good doctor had already turned him down flat. "I'll consider it. Thanks, Debra."

"I'll talk with you tomorrow. Chin up."

Cole ended the call. What in the hell was he going to do?

He let himself consider seducing Dr. Finley for two seconds longer than he should. He knew he couldn't do it. Not only would it feel wrong to him, a woman with her intellect would never let it happen and he would end up looking like a love-starved idiot. Again. In the short time he'd known her he knew what she would and would not accept in certain situations. And a love affair was probably at the top of her list of things to avoid.

There would be no flattery, flirting or sucking up with Dr. Finley because if he tried he knew she would call him on it. He was drawn to her, his body responding immediately and decisively every time he got close. At those times she could ask him to fly to the moon and he would do it. He had to get a grip on the attraction, step back from her and the situation.

He sat back in his desk chair, took a deep breath then rubbed his hands together, an old habit he had any time he was perplexed about something. Somehow he had to get her out of there, at least for the day of the ground-breaking. Surely she would agree once she understood the necessity.

He could offer to extend the ninety days in exchange for her agreeing to disappear next weekend. It would delay his project even further but at this point, what was another few days? The impression he made next week was vitally important. His plan had been to have the foundations poured and some of the framing completed on the main lodge structure. So much for that idea. All he could do now was pick up the pieces and go from there. And the last thing he needed was Tallie there distracting him when so much was on the line.

* * *

The next day when Cole pulled his truck up to the site, she kept working. For a man who wanted her off his property he certainly spent an exorbitant amount of time at the dig.

"Good morning," he said, smiling.

Tallie couldn't tell if his greeting was forced but she had an inkling he was after something. What was it this time?

"You moved where you're working."

She didn't give the man the benefit of an answer.

"Didn't you?"

With a huffed sigh, she embedded the shovel into the ground and faced the horrible man. "Yes. I moved out of the mud."

"I hope your instincts are right," he said. "Too bad if you spent all this time for nothing."

Tallie chose to remain quiet.

"What's this?" Cole walked over to the sifter, obviously choosing to ignore her cold shoulder. "Is it broken?"

"That's my sifting box and, no, it isn't broken. I normally use it in a plowed field but I decided to try it here. It speeds up the process especially since someone kindly provided me with thoroughly churned dirt. The negative is I run the risk of damaging a relic."

She demonstrated by jabbing the narrow shovel into the earth, used her foot to send it a bit farther into the red soil then dumped her load into the sifter. "Now you shake it and look for anything unnatural left in the tray. Anything you think shouldn't be in there. It could be unusually shaped rocks, onions or other roots from a past garden, or of course, painted pottery, arrow heads, jewelry…"

"Jewelry?"

"Just because people lived five or six thousand years ago doesn't mean the ladies didn't want to look their best."

"Five *thousand* years?" Cole was surprised. "You're attempting to find something from a culture that old?"

"That's the plan. According to my grandmother, our ancestors' tribe dates back that far. But it doesn't matter because it's none of your concern," she replied, keeping her voice calm even though she was flustered. She seemed to constantly be flustered around this man. Thankfully, the little butterflies in her stomach remained on the inside out of sight. "Anyway, how can I help you this morning?" If she had a door, she would help him through it.

He seemed to hesitate; his hands coming to rest on his hips while he appeared to stare into space. "I need a favor," he said, shifting his gaze to her face.

"A favor? From *me*?" She couldn't keep the sarcastic tone from her voice. "This should be good."

"There's a ground-breaking ceremony scheduled for next Friday. I have CEOs from various companies coming in from all over the country. They are interested in investing in my project and want to see it. What little there is of it."

"And you need me to disappear."

His eyebrows rose in surprise, as though he hadn't expected her to understand so quickly. "Friday, if you wouldn't mind?"

She stopped shaking the sifter and faced him, one hand on her hip. "You need to make up your mind. You call my boss and insist I work faster. Now you're asking me to stop working altogether." She shook her head. "Can I know why you want me to stop my work? I mean, what I'm doing is perfectly legal. It's certainly nothing to be ashamed of. In fact it's been my experience that most people are fascinated by what we do. Normally we lose a couple of hours a day from having to stop and give demonstrations or explanations of exactly what we hope to find and how we go about finding it."

"So, you're refusing?"

The bullheaded man obviously hadn't heard one word she'd said. She shook her head and absently pulled the banana clip from her hair. She finger-combed her locks, twisted the length back into a scruffy knot and replaced the clip.

"I'll try and work in an area as remote and out of sight of your guests as possible on that day. But I can't stop working completely. I'm sure it never occurred to you, but I want to go home as badly as you want me to. But this isn't over until I find proof of what I'm looking for or run out of time."

"Even if I extended your ninety days by another four days to make up for it?"

She shook her head. "The day after I finish here I'm on a flight to Brazil." At least that had been the plan before an egotistical, drop-dead gorgeous male had gotten her pregnant. "I just don't see any need to stop if I stay out of the way." She pointed to an area on the other side of a shallow ravine. "I'll work over there while your group is here, but that's all I'm willing to do. I cannot lose a full day of work."

"How about if I call you before we get here and you disappear for an hour or so?"

That would work. She nodded her head and provided him with her cell number.

Today Cole wore a T-shirt, his biceps stretching the short sleeves; a slight smattering of dark hair peeked over the top of the neckline. The jeans he wore were not skintight but it was still easy to see the muscles. They made his legs appear slightly bowed, which seemed to emphasize his sexuality. Well-worn Western boots completed the effect. Which was all undoubtedly part of his plan. Dress down. Talk to her on her lower level. She could appreciate the effort but it didn't work. God! If he would just stop the stupid sneak attacks and be open and straightforward about things.

But she had to admit, whatever he wore, he was temptation run amok. With his almost golden eyes, thick, dark hair and full lips begging to be kissed, he could easily have most women falling at his feet. He could never know how close she was to giving in and running into his arms. She wanted that and more. And how stupid would that be? Cole Masters made her ex look like an amateur by comparison.

Good grief. She pushed such thoughts away. She

had to focus on her work and keep her imagination at bay. Still…it was next to impossible to not imagine his arms around her, his lips on hers as he explored deeper inside her mouth, his touch scorching her skin. She envied the beautiful women who drew him like a hummingbird to nectar. But she would never be one of those women. She'd be wise to remember that.

A week later Tallie still hadn't found anything. That morning she slept in. Not that she did it on purpose. She'd always used her internal clock, which was amazingly accurate but apparently had failed to work this time. Cole Masters had turned off the alarm. Her dreams had been filled with him and that bothered her.

Yawning, she thought about her next steps. Toward the cliffs. She just had a feeling if there was ever a tribe in this immediate area, it would be within a fairly small radius of the cliffs. Prepared for surprises, she always began her digs at the furthermost spot and worked her way in. Now, with time growing ever shorter, she needed to move faster, take bigger steps to where the heart of the village might have been. The area where she would stake out yet another grid was still within the field of wheat but would edge her much closer to the sharp incline at the foot of the mesa. If there had been caves in the cliffs at some time in the past, there had to be remnants of a society below.

An hour later, after finishing her tea, she was on

her way to the site to set up another grid. It took a couple hours before Tallie tossed her first shovelful of soil from the new area into the sifter. And an hour later still, all she'd found were rocks and some pottery splinters. They were definitely old and came from deeper in the ground than the other remnants she'd found, which was promising. Unfortunately she didn't have the equipment or the software to determine age. That would require a lab. All she could do was make a best guess.

As she began to shake the dirt from the wire screen, a flash of light caught her attention. Glancing over to the tracks behind the cabin she saw a line of limos turning into the gates of the property, headed in the general direction of the cabin. *Crap.* Was this Friday? As usual she'd lost all track of time.

Why hadn't Cole called? That was the plan. Cole was to give her a one-hour heads-up. Reaching into her pocket she pulled out her cell. No bars. She had no reception. She stared at the phone in shock. Cole's guests had arrived. And even after the stunts he'd pulled, she believed in keeping her word. She'd told him she would disappear for a couple of hours and she would do it.

She glanced around her, making sure all of her equipment was out of sight. She was lower than the trapper shack, giving them a better view of her than she had of them. Thankfully everything looked to be as camouflaged as was possible. The sifter was the only obvious tool and there was no time to tear it down.

The cars were slowly approaching the gate to the property fifty yards from the shack. *The shack.* She'd forgotten to clear her things out of the old cabin. Would they look inside? She did a quick mental calculation. She might have time to remove her belongings before the motorcade got to Cole's project site. She'd also have to move her old Ford wagon, which was parked right next to the shack. If they even slowed down, they would know someone was working in the area.

She tossed the shovel into the hole and hurried to the old trapper's cabin. Sprinting up the steps and into the building, she grabbed an armful of clothes and headed back out to throw them into the wagon. The bedroll and pillow were next. She had just cleared the last of her personal items from in and around the rickety old building and shut the Ford's door when the first limo drove past. She darted back inside the shack, having no clue what to do now. Maybe no one would come over. They had no reason to. Backing into the corner next to the window opening, she silently watched as several more limos eased past. Could she slowly back her vehicle out of here without anyone knowing?

The dig was in the opposite direction from the shack and his project site. If she could sneak out the door and get to the oak tree, maybe she could nonchalantly stroll back to her dig? The current excavation was deep enough to provide cover if she could make it there. But she immediately nixed that idea.

Better not to take a chance. She would stay where she was and hope no one noticed.

Tallie could hear Cole's voice as he explained his vision for the corporate retreat center he was planning, answering questions and fielding concerns. Then there were a few chuckles, which should be a good sign, but nothing in Cole's voice indicated he was laughing. More to the point, it sounded as if he'd been put on the defensive. Dare she peek at the small group to see what was happening? Curiosity overcame her. Easing over to the doorway, she peeked out in time to see several people in the group pointing toward her dig.

Oh, man. She withdrew inside the cabin. Everything outside got quiet. What was happening? She didn't want to sabotage Cole or his project. She didn't have the same ruthless character he did. His project was as important to him as her dig was to her. She went back over the actions she'd taken since first seeing the limos start to arrive. She was certain no one had seen her dumping clothes and tools in her wagon. She was done before the first car had topped the small rise. So what was going on out there?

She again stepped over to the door, peered around the corner and came face-to-face with Cole. He was definitely not a happy camper. Though his features were still handsome, his eyes narrowed, honing in on her. She pulled back then took a couple of steps further inside the cabin. She felt like an animal caught in a trap. When he stepped inside, the space in the small room seemed to evaporate. His shoulders were so wide he had to turn slightly sideways to enter; his head was mere inches from the ceiling rafters. His full lips were pulled into a straight line. She never thought she would see him angrier than he'd been that first day. She'd been wrong.

"Your presence is requested outside," he said. "It appears digging a hole is more interesting than any project I could come up with. Would you mind coming out and addressing the group of investors?"

"You're kidding." Her voice was gone; a whisper was the best she could do. "Tell me you're joking! Everything is stashed out of sight except..."

"The sifter," they both said at once.

"Why didn't you leave?" he asked in an angry whisper.

"Because I never got your call," she snapped, equally mad. "You should have known there would be no cell service down there."

"Me?"

"Yes, *you*!"

"You're the one digging over there."

"It's not my land."

"You couldn't prove that by me," he huffed. "Come on. Might as well give them some reason for being here."

She took a deep breath and blew it out, shaking her head at the irony. One small sifter on forty thousand acres and that's what they wanted to see. She glanced down at her bare legs and shorts. The worn T-shirt added to the effect. "I'm not appropriately dressed."

Cole's eyebrows went straight up. "Dr. Finley, that is the least of your worries." He walked back outside and turned around. "Are you coming?"

Nine

Tallie didn't want to go out there and address his potential investors, and the temptation to be stubborn almost won out. But, taking a deep breath, she removed the banana clip from her hair and quickly brushed it out. When she stepped outside there were approximately twenty people, men and women, all standing under the giant oak tree, and everyone was smiling. Everyone except Cole Masters.

"This is Dr. Tallie Finley, archaeologist with the North Texas Natural History Museum. She has degrees in biological and forensic anthropology. She's agreed to take a few minutes and answer your questions."

Without any hesitation the questions started coming hard and heavy but she'd heard them all before.

Many times. They were talking her language now and she felt herself start to relax. Most people were intrigued by the recovery of ancient artifacts but very few got to visit an actual dig. She could feel the investors' excitement building.

"We're looking for relics dating back about five or six thousand years. We received some evidence that a tribe once lived in this area. Mr. Masters was... *gracious* enough to let us come in and search, even though doing so delayed his own project."

Tallie didn't dare look at Cole, who stood next to her. "If we find what we're looking for, it could change the way we understand Native American history and culture, including my own lineage. We, at the museum, are holding our breath, we're so excited about this site."

Excitement spurred the crowd to ask more questions. Eventually someone asked to see where she was now digging. They followed Tallie down the small incline to the two large square holes.

After explaining the various tools and how they were used, Tallie reached down and picked up a tea can, tumbling a few objects onto the sifter so all could see. She picked one dark gray rock and held it up. "So far I've found several of these. The arrowheads were attached to sticks or poles and used for hunting." She put down the rock and picked up several pieces of pottery. "This is evidence that a village was here. We can scan these pieces and, with today's technology, the computer can give us a realistic idea of the size of the actual pot and, in some cases, what it was used for."

"Isn't that what you're looking for?" someone asked.

"No." She smiled and shook her head. "These are relatively new. Only a few hundred years old."

Everyone chuckled. Except Cole.

Tallie tossed the pieces back into the sifting tray and walked over to an odd-shaped rock, round on one end with a long, narrow stem on the other, sitting near a small shrub. "This we found yesterday." She was careful to use "we" instead of "I," implying a much bigger operation. "It was used to grind corn and wheat." She held it up for them to see. "And, yes, this, too, is only a few hundred years old."

The questions continued: How did she know the age of the samples? What kind of artifact did she hope to find that bore evidence of something five thousand years old? How long would this dig go on? What part did Cole play in all of this?

"If it were not for Mr. Masters, we wouldn't have any chance at obtaining the necessary proof." That much was true, even if it had taken a court order to search there.

She glanced at Cole. His face was unreadable. But his lips were pursed as though he was holding back a grin. Why would he do that?

The questions continued for several more minutes then eventually died off.

"If no one has any more questions, let's return to the house where a late luncheon is waiting." Cole directed them up the slight hill and back to the limos. Before following, he stepped over to Tallie. "You and I are going to have a talk."

"No problem. Name the place and the time." If he thought he could intimidate her, he could think again. He was not so different than John, who walked into a room as though he owned it. The only difference was that Cole actually did own this property.

"I'm curious. Where did you learn to lie so well?"

"I didn't lie." She shrugged. "I just didn't go into too much detail in my answers. And it just seemed like the right thing to do. Have a good afternoon."

Lively sparks lit his brown eyes and that said a lot. Just what, exactly, she didn't know. But she was ready. She had formed tough armor long ago when she was in school. *So bring it on.*

He looked at her for another few seconds, pursed his lips again and shook his head before turning and walking away.

Tallie finished a quadrant and hung her head. Sitting back, her elbows bracing her shoulders, she asked herself what she was doing wrong. The top few layers of soil had not given up any secrets. Not surprising. Most of what she was searching for was so old it would be covered under several layers of dirt. Erosion, windstorms, flooding, any number of weather-related changes could move soil up or down or to a different location, making it harder to find what she was looking for. It was like stirring batter in a mixing bowl. The question was: where to go next? And how? Lately, she was starting to feel uncomfortable lying on her stomach. She certainly didn't want to do anything to hurt her baby.

She rose, looking at the red earthen cliff less than a hundred yards away. Shielding her eyes from the lowering sun, Tallie again scoured the embankment, alert to any signs of caves or stacked rocks. There were a couple of places that piqued her interest but getting to them wouldn't be a walk in the park. She would continue her search down here. She reasoned if anyone had lived up in the cliffs, they would have surely had to throw something down at some point. So she would keep looking on the ground.

The sun was setting on another day. She would move her exploration to the north, just below the dark spot on the cliff face. How she wished her grandmother was here so that she could ask her any number of questions. When she got back to camp, she would study the map again. Maybe she'd missed something.

She felt sick. She hurried away from the grid and dropped to her knees. She was so tired and the daily sickness seemed to zap the last bit of strength from her. A small part of her wanted to break down and cry—but she clamped down hard on those emotions.

As she walked back to the cabin her thoughts were of Cole. Sooner or later she would have to tell him about the baby. It was beginning to be impossible to snap her jeans, so she'd need some new clothing that would doubtlessly show her pregnancy. How would he take the news? What would he do?

Would he accuse her of getting pregnant on purpose or would he be happy?

A sadness in her heart told her he probably wouldn't. Would he deny it was his? She almost wished he would. She'd loved the night they shared. She didn't want to have the memories of that night tainted by ugly accusations and anger. She longed for him to accept her; to accept the baby. But it was not reality. The most she could hope for was to complete her assignment as quickly as possible then leave with him being none the wiser.

Deep inside where no one could see, she'd given the mysterious stranger in New Orleans a small piece of her heart. Now, knowing the true identity of the man didn't change that at all. She remembered the sparkle in both of her parents' eyes when they were together. It was pure devotion; there was never a thought of anyone else. She doubted that dream would ever be hers. Especially with someone like Cole Masters. He was too handsome, too powerful. The epitome of a perfect male. He was everything she'd ever dreamed of. Her and a million other women. She needed to find the proof she was after and leave before she fell in love with a man who would never, *could* never, love her back.

The meeting had gone exceedingly well and while Cole was reluctant to admit it, in large part it was thanks to Tallie. Watching her address the guests, her long hair flowing down her back, and that incredible smile on her beautiful face, he realized she'd been right when she'd said people were curious about her work.

The conversation over lunch was lively, the topics ranging from his project to her dig to Masters Corporation. Cole avoided these last questions, needing the prospective investors to know from the get-go that his project had nothing to do with the family business. Most understood, or said they did, and were okay with it. Then Tallie's search for pottery or whatever she was looking for inched its way back into the conversation.

Several investors told him before leaving that if he was willing to go to such lengths to bring history alive, they had every confidence in his ability to bring his own project to fruition. And they'd all pledged they were on board. In one afternoon, Tallie had helped make his anxiety vanish. And for that, Cole was in her debt.

Tallie Finley was living in dangerous conditions. She could joke about finding the grass snake in her shoe but what would happen when she woke up one morning to find a rattlesnake coiled in the corner of the small shack or under the rusty old bed? He didn't like the odds of her coming away from this dig unscathed. And although signed disclaimers said differently, he felt ultimately responsible. If she wouldn't see reason and leave, it was up to him to ensure her living environment was as safe as he could make it. Staying at the ranch house was the ideal solution. If he was honest with himself, that idea had as much to do with his libido as it did with her safety, but he'd see to it safety concerns were addressed nonetheless.

He'd told her they needed to talk after the investors left. And he wanted to see her; to thank her for her participation and the positive way she'd handled the situation.

Once everyone was gone, Cole bounded up the stairs and changed into jeans and a plaid shirt. He was going to drive out and personally thank Tallie for her assistance. She'd made the difference. When he was dressed, he walked outside and jumped in the truck and headed for Tallie's dig.

It was a beautiful evening for a ride. He should have taken one of the horses, but he'd been in a hurry. A sensation akin to panic urged him to get to her as quickly as possible. He didn't question the why of it.

When Cole drove up to the little cabin he didn't immediately see her. Once more, a little twinge of concern nipped at his senses although why he didn't know.

He walked around to the front of the shack and peeked inside. She wasn't there. He took in the bedroll spread over a nasty mattress on a rusty bed that should have been thrown out years ago. A bird darted out the window. The rays of the setting sun lit the holes in the ceiling. He still couldn't believe she'd been living in this pathetic excuse for a shelter. Glancing toward the river, he spotted two jeans-clad legs under a tree. Sure enough, Tallie leaned against a giant tree trunk, sound asleep. Her hands

were pressed together, palm to palm, making a pillow for her head.

When he got to her, Cole couldn't resist reaching out and smoothing her hair back from her brow.
She felt hot. Not surprising, given the triple-digit
temperatures. But dehydration was not something
to be taken lightly.

"Tallie?" He squatted next to her. "Tallie?"

She responded by sitting up and stretching while
taking a deep breath. Every nerve ending in his body
sat up and took notice. Damn, she was hot. In more
ways than one.

She gazed at him, blinking twice then shooting
up like he'd thrown cold water in her face. For a
few seconds she staggered, fighting to keep her balance and wake up. The surprise showed clearly in
those radiant green eyes. Then she looked away and
rubbed her hands over her face.

"Have you been drinking plenty of water?"

She nodded. "Yeah. I'm just really tired and I
guess I fell asleep. I came down here because it's so
hot at the dig." She chanced a glance in his direction.

Cole stood. Her voice was husky from sleep, a
definite turn-on.

"But I'm making progress. I—"

Suddenly she staggered a short distance away
from him, fell to her knees and proceeded to be sick.
Cole honestly didn't know what to do. He walked
over to her and pulled her long hair back from her
face. By the time the nausea passed, she was trembling.

"Do you need a doctor?"

"No. I mean it's okay. I must have picked up a bug." She sat back, resting her head on her raised knees. "I'm sorry about that."

"No apologies necessary. Let's get you to the house. You need a few hours out of this heat. No arguments."

Her slender nose flared and the muscles in her jaw tightened as though his suggestion made her angry. What had he said? She quickly brought whatever had bothered her under control.

"Thanks, but I really should stay with the dig. I'm now behind several hours." She turned toward him, still not meeting his eyes. "I really am doing my best to get out of your way. I can't quit. What may be here is too important."

"I promise I won't hold it against you if you take the afternoon and evening off. You've been at this solid for weeks."

She nodded.

"Come to dinner. Take a refreshing shower or soak in the tub—whatever makes you feel better. Get out of this heat for a while and put something in your stomach besides Cocoa Puffs and peanut butter and crackers."

That earned him a glance. He found himself holding his breath.

Finally she nodded. "Okay. If you're sure. That would be great. Thanks."

No woman he'd ever met could pass up a hot bath. And food was probably an equally important enticement under these circumstances. It was not helping his cause to feed and care for the enemy. But he couldn't let her work herself to death. He believed she was giving it her all. And he owed her for making him look good in front of his investors.

"Grab some clean clothes and anything else you need to take and let's go."

"Now?"

"Now," he confirmed. "Before you change your mind."

When they got to the mansion, they parked in the allotted area and headed to the French doors in the back. The coolness of the air-conditioned room was a welcome relief as were the cold marble tiles under her feet. It was such a great feeling she didn't want to go any farther.

"Do you remember the way to the suite you used the last time?" he asked softly.

"Yes, thank you."

Looking around, she remembered the enormous, eight-foot-wide, natural-stone fireplace that rose to the ceiling of the three-story home. Huge log beams crossed the room just below the ceiling. The entire bottom floor was open, which made it seem even bigger. But it was the kitchen that really took her breath away. A bronze exhaust fan overshadowed the five-burner stove and copper pots and pans hung from a rack above the enormous marble-topped island in the center of the room. An oak table sat in a large area off to the side of the kitchen. The view out the floor-to-ceiling windows was incredible. It was a sight similar to the one she had from the trapper's shack, only from an elevation and a lot more dramatic.

After a wonderful massage in the jetted tub, shampooing her hair and putting on fresh clothes she felt invigorated. Gathering her dirty T-shirt and jeans into a bundle, she brushed out her hair and headed downstairs. The aroma of the food was the next thing to heaven. Cole met her as she entered the kitchen, holding a plastic bag for her laundry. With the light still dancing in his eyes, he handed her a glass of wine.

"You look like a new person," he said as his eyes roamed over the sundress she'd put on. "Very nice."

She knew it was stupid but she hadn't wanted to wear her work clothes. She'd wanted to dress up a little. And it was just a *little*. She'd brought plenty of shorts and jeans and, for reasons she would never understand, she'd thrown the white-lace sundress into the bag along with her sandals. Now here she was, standing in the home of a billionaire in a twenty-dollar dress she'd picked up from a discount store. She supposed stranger things happened to some people but this was it for her.

"Thanks," she said. "That bath was amazing. It's not often we are invited by the local residents to come into their home and experience some twenty-first-century innovations."

"You mean like indoor plumbing?" His eyes sparkled with humor.

"Exactly. I'm almost afraid to ask, but how did the meeting go? Hopefully they all signed up to give their support."

"They did, as a matter of fact. And it was in a large part thanks to you." He caught her gaze and held it. "I appreciate it, Tallie."

"Excuse me, sir," the chef interrupted. "Your dinner is served in the breakfast nook, as requested."

Cole nodded to Andre and turned to her, asking, "Are you hungry?"

"Not really, although it smells delicious." She placed a hand over her stomach. Then, realizing it would draw attention, she quickly let her hand drop to her side.

"Still feeling sick?"

"Maybe a little."

With a hand on her lower back that felt both comforting and strange he guided her through the great room, kitchen and finally to the dining area.

Tallie was surprised to see the room lit only with the glow from a large candle in the center of the table. Suddenly she wished she hadn't accepted the invitation to come to dinner. This had seduction written all over it and she would never fall into that trap again. She couldn't even imagine what a woman would feel on the day Cole Masters decided he wanted to move on. Especially if the woman imagined herself in love with him. But more than likely all Cole wanted was to find out more about the dig and any loopholes that he could use to make her leave. It had nothing to do with her personally.

Remember that.

Cole held out her chair. From this angle she could see the waterfall and the floral display highlighted by hidden lights. Lowering himself into a chair next to hers, he smiled as though glad to have her there. She attempted to smile back. But this wasn't some nice neighbor like old Ben Weatherly down the street where she lived.

She appreciated the bath. She would certainly appreciate a few bites of the delicious food that had just been set in front of her. But she was not stopping her dig. If that was his intention with all of this, he could have well saved his efforts. It would take a lot more than a gourmet dinner and some kiss-up dialogue to make her change her mind.

"So, have you discovered anything remotely interesting as yet?"

She shook her head, trying to keep her eyes from rolling at the question. "Not yet."

"I'm curious. Don't they usually send more than one person on an important dig like this?"

"Yes, they do. I'm here by myself because of budget constraints and because I was the one who provided the map."

He looked surprised. "You found that map?"

She nodded.

"Do you mind if I ask where?"

"It was given to me by my grandmother. Just before she died."

"So she isn't here to provide any answers."

"Exactly. I don't know why she waited. I don't

know if she had any more information about where to look. Or specifically what I'm looking for. Everything but the map died with her."

"I'm sorry for your loss."

He was quiet for a while. Tallie knew he was debating if he should ask any more questions. She hoped he didn't. She didn't exactly know what she could tell him.

"This is really delicious," she said, making a valiant effort to change the subject.

He produced a smile that lit up his face. "Thanks. Beef stroganoff is one of my favorites, although I tend to like German food the most. What's your preference?"

"Cocoa Puffs and peanut butter," she answered with a completely straight face.

He laughed. "I guess that puts this a few notches down on the list."

"Well, like steak or lobster, it'll do in a pinch."

"Next time, I'll know what to serve."

Next time? Would there be a next time? She very much doubted it. This was his chance to use his persuasive powers to make her give up the dig. Most likely he wouldn't show her such hospitality again. She just had to get through tonight and perhaps he would leave her alone for a while.

"I feel good about the grid I'm working now. It's close to the cliffs and it looks like there may have been caves in that area at one time."

"And that's important?"

She nodded. "Ancient people often lived in caves.

They were nature's way of providing the best refuge against the elements, wild animals and other tribes. I scanned the cliff face with the binoculars but couldn't see anything resembling an opening, even a small one."

"I hope for your sake you find something soon."

He must have seen the disbelief cross her face.

"No. I mean it. The temperature isn't getting any cooler. I can't believe they expect one person to pick her way through acres of land to find a piece of pottery or whatever it is you're hoping to find. You've been here for almost two months. I know you have to be getting anxious to get back to your home."

Tallie hoped he was a better negotiator over a conference table. He apparently didn't know the definition of the word subtle.

"Most of the digs I'm assigned take six to eight months. The number-one requirement for an archeologist is patience. Nothing ever happens fast or on a schedule."

"You must really love what you do."

"I'd better, huh?" She grinned at him and he looked stunned, as though someone had held up a cream pie and threatened to smash it in his face. "The hope of what you'll uncover in the next grid is such a rush. And once you start finding things, you just have to go for the next and the next. I guess to some people it's addictive."

"Are you addicted, Tallie?"

His question in that deep, raspy voice caught her by surprise and drew her gaze to his. It was almost as though he hadn't meant to ask it out loud. He sat back in his chair, one arm resting on the other, and idly drew his thumb back and forth across his bottom lip while he waited for her answer. Her gaze dropped to the movement and his mouth. What would it be like to give herself to him completely now that they knew each other? Now that she knew who he was? What would he do? What *wouldn't* he do?

A picture flashed in her mind of pure, red-hot passion, tangled sheets and Cole's lips lingering a breath above hers as he moved deeper inside her. Tallie felt the singeing warmth flooding the area between her legs at the thought. The image became so clear, her stomach tightened in knots. Everything about him was so sexy. His handsome face alone would cause most women to feel the overwhelming need to be with him. He looked at a woman with those golden eyes and it made her want to toss any thought of saying no out the window. He was sex personified. All he needed to do was breathe.

Suddenly realizing what she was doing, she quickly looked away. Had he intended her to gaze at his lips? While the entire experience could not have lasted a full minute, her heart was beating out of her chest and her breathing was almost nonexistent. Laying her fork on the edge of her plate, she tried to control her eyes, not wanting to see if he was smiling or mocking her. Even though she didn't know him well at all, the thought that it might be the latter would be hard to take.

She blotted the linen napkin against her mouth.

"This was really delicious. And the bath was great. Thank you, Cole."

"Stay, Tallie," he said as she moved to get up from the table. "Stay here tonight. Sleep in a clean bed. No bugs, raccoons or skunks. No heat." He dropped his napkin on the table and looked directly at her. "Unless you want there to be."

Tallie swallowed hard and felt a blush roll up her neck and over her face. She knew what he was suggesting but she didn't know if he was serious or teasing. And she didn't know how to answer.

"I'd better get back to the site," she said as she stood. "But, again, thanks for sharing your home. I feel much better."

Cole rounded the table to stand in front of her. "Why do you insist on sleeping in that shack? You can't possibly be resting well. No one could. Stay here, your choice of bedrooms, and drive to your dig each morning. It makes sense. It's a big house, so neither of us will be tripping over the other." He reached out and tilted her chin to meet his gaze. "It makes sense, Tallie."

She saw a glimmer of passion in his amazing eyes. She'd seen that glimmer before. She wanted to stay. She wanted him. Clearly he was only too happy to oblige. He leaned over and placed his lips on hers. She didn't move away. Encouraged, he encircled her with his arms and pulled her closer. She could feel his erection against her belly and that sent a stream of heat rushing to her core.

"I need you, Tallie," he whispered against her

ear. "God help me, I can't stay away." He advanced, pushing her against the wall, threading her fingers with his behind her back. "Give us a chance. This time, no games. We'll both be up front. Make love to me."

Cole knew exactly where to touch, how to kiss to make her entire world spin out of control in a way that was good and wild and exciting. He was temptation run amuck. And she craved it. She'd heard stories of hot, steamy sex, of the climax that made you feel you were flying up to the stars, but she had never felt that sense of completion until one sultry night in New Orleans. "I'm flattered, really. But I'd better get back to my dig." She let go of his hands, breaking the physical tie between them.

"My intentions are not to flatter you. Take me off the damn pedestal, Tallie. I'm just a man. A man who wants you. Who needs you. You make me feel like no other woman ever has."

It was hard to argue with a man who towered over her with a look on his face of pure sincerity and a voice to back it up. Tallie closed her eyes, inhaling the scent of pure male, and her body responded accordingly, leaving her wanting to ask only where he wanted her.

Her eyes fluttered open and she stepped away. She'd almost done it again: succumbed to him and his desire. He was merely taking advantage of a situation that had landed in his lap. She believed he meant no harm, but the man had a reputation with the ladies and in business circles she'd heard he could be ruthless. If she took him up on the offer, she would feel awkward to still be stuck with having to deal with him until the ninety days on the site were up.

Without any warning, the room began to spin. She reached out for something to steady herself and found Cole's arm. "I… I think I'm going to—" Blackness surrounded her.

Ten

Tallie awakened on the sofa in the spacious den. A cool, damp cloth was being pressed against her forehead.

"Hey." Cole's voice called to her. "There you are."

Tallie didn't have time for small talk. Nausea was hitting hard and fast.

"Bathroom." She sat up. "Where is…?"

Cole stood, clearly looking concerned. "Down that hall on the right."

Tallie prayed she would make it in time as she lit out like a bottle rocket. When the worst was over, Cole stood ready to hand her a damp washcloth. Tallie dropped to the bathroom floor, too weak to move.

"Let's get you to a place you can lie down." Without another word, he scooped her up into his arms as though she weighed nothing.

"I'm so sorry I upset the dinner. I lost that great dinner."

"Don't worry about it."

He laid her gently on a huge bed in one of the bedrooms. The en suite bath was close by.

"Thank you," she said and closed her eyes. She couldn't think about the embarrassment of what had happened. She would have to face that tomorrow.

She must have dozed. She awoke sometime later with a kind-looking, gray-haired man sitting in a chair next to the bed. Cole hovered in the doorway.

"Tallie, I am Dr. Jenkins," the man introduced himself. "Can you tell me what happened?"

"We, uh, we had dinner. I stood up when we were finished and the room started spinning. Next thing I knew it was lights out. When I woke up I was exceedingly nauseous. I feel better now, though still a little queasy. It's probably just a two-day bug or something. No reason to bother you."

"You are most likely right about the virus, but since I'm already here, let's find out, okay?" He smiled. He was so gentle and reassuring Tallie couldn't help but agree. "Cole," the doctor said without looking toward the door, "please close the door on your way out."

The door was closed without any protest.

"Now, let's start with your lungs. Can you sit forward and take some deep breaths?"

He checked her lungs, looked in her eyes and throat. "Have you been feeling sluggish?"

"No."

"Any fever?"

"No. Not that I know of."

"Any other stomach-related virus?"

"No."

"Okay." The doctor returned his instruments to his bag. "One last question," he said. "Could you be pregnant?"

Tallie could feel the blood drain from her face. She should have anticipated the question. She had been with one man. And that man was no doubt standing on the other side of the door.

"I didn't mean to upset you, my dear," the doctor said, concern covering his face. "It's definitely a personal question. I mention it only because all the symptoms you described fit. How about you come by the office tomorrow and we can run a test and be absolutely certain?"

"Okay," she agreed. But Tallie knew he was right. She had already seen an OB-GYN. Today wasn't the first time she'd felt that wave of nausea. She was pregnant and Cole was the only man who could be the father. And she knew he would not be pleased. And that was an understatement.

"Dr. Jenkins," she said, "please don't say anything to Cole about your suspicions. I'm an archeologist here for a limited amount of time. If he thought I was…well, he might make me leave and my work here is highly important." There was no way she would tell anyone who the father was, especially Cole and his doctor. Schemer. Tramp. Gold digger. Con artist. The insults she'd face would be endless. She just had to wrap up her work as quickly as possible and leave.

"I would never discuss a patient's health with anyone without prior written approval," he assured her. "But I must advise you, if you are with child, working outdoors in this heat could cause complications. It's a very realistic possibility that you could lose the baby."

That didn't help to calm her racing heart.

"Shall I let Cole come back in? I know he is worried."

She nodded; after all, she would have to face him sooner or later. "That's fine."

As soon as the good doctor left the room she was out of the bed, had her shoes on and was ready to walk out behind him. Cole met her at the door.

"I'm fine," she said, unable to look him in the face. "Sorry I caused you so much trouble."

"Where are you going?"

"Back to the dig site. I imagine it's late and everyone wants to get to sleep."

"I'm everyone. And I don't want you going back out there tonight. If you want, I can have some men stand guard over your things, but you need to have some time to hydrate and chill out under the air conditioning."

"I'll be fine."

"Did the doctor say what he thinks it is? Why you collapsed? Why you got sick?"

"He wasn't sure. Probably a virus I picked up somewhere."

Cole was looking at her with suspicion written all over his face. She had to get out of there and go somewhere she could be alone and sort all this out.

"I insist you remain here at least for the night. We can talk about future accommodations later."

She was torn between wanting to be away from him and wanting to stay in his home. To say it was very comfortable was an understatement. To sleep on fresh, cool, silk sheets atop a mattress as soft as a cloud was beyond tempting. But the longer she remained in his presence, the more tempting it was to come clean about the baby.

"Tallie, it's the right thing to do and I think you know that."

"Fine. Okay," she said. "But just for tonight."

"Good. No more badgering then, but we are going to discuss this. You need to sleep here from now on."

"I appreciate the loan of the shirt," she said, choosing to ignore his other statement.

Later, as she lay in bed inhaling the rich, relaxing scent of the linen spray, she wished she could remain here. But Cole would discover her secret soon enough without pushing it in his face. She would, therefore, remain at the old shack and hope she would find the relics she needed sooner than later.

* * *

She was up early. Dressed in the white sundress, she headed down the stairs. A woman in a maid's uniform met her in the kitchen.

"Good morning, ma'am. Would you care for a fresh cup of coffee or tea?"

Do bears have hair? "Tea would be wonderful. Is it possible I might also get a piece of dry toast?"

"Certainly, ma'am," the woman replied as she poured the tea into a large mug.

Tallie slipped onto a bar stool and added sugar and cream to the tea. She took a sip; the tea was amazingly good, better than what she could make for herself. Maybe before she left to return home she could find out the brand. It was definitely worth asking.

"She found the tea." Cole's voice came from behind her. She turned in her chair to face him. "How are you feeling this morning?"

"Much better, thank you. Cole, I am so sorry that I—"

"Stop. I'm just glad it was nothing serious."

Tallie swallowed hard and nodded her head. How serious was being pregnant? She knew in that moment she should tell him but couldn't bring herself to do it. Not here. Not now.

Cole slid into the chair next to her and sipped his own tea while Tallie ate her toast. She needed to get back to the dig while the temperature was still cool.

"I need to fly to Houston this morning," Cole told

her. "I'm going to trust that you won't work so hard that your body overheats again."

"I won't."

"Good."

"I'll be back by six or seven. Consider moving into the big house. I don't want you sleeping out there with no telling what. Raccoons, at the very least."

"I'll be fine." She smiled at him. "I certainly don't want to intrude in a bachelor's domain."

"You would only make it better." He leaned down for a kiss and, with renewed promises he would see her later, finished the last of his tea and walked with her to his truck.

While Cole was in Houston, she wanted to get back to work. That was the only thing that seemed real and solid.

Half an hour later she had changed into shorts and a T-shirt and was busy mapping out a new grid. She loved working with the soil, the rich scent of the earth a heady reminder of what might be buried below. It was easy to get lost in her work and lose track of time, even when she wasn't really finding anything. The next thing she knew, when she paused and looked up from the dirt she was sifting, the sun was already low on the horizon.

She'd just stepped inside the old cabin at the end of the day when her cell phone began to ring. Her eyebrows went up in surprise to see Stan Bridger's name flash across the screen.

"Hey, you," she said, smiling. "It's about time

you came home." Stan had been on a dig in central Mexico for the past three months.

"You will get no argument from me," he replied.

Stan was a good friend who had initially been the deciding factor in her choice to major in archeology. Several years her senior, he had helped her attain her Ph.D., cheered her on when she'd landed a job with the museum and stayed with her during most of her first dig. He'd taught her about all the documents required and the basic day-to-day operation on a dig. She had a sneaking suspicion he'd been partially responsible for her getting the job, but he wouldn't admit it and she couldn't prove it. As the months passed she'd let it drop. It no longer mattered. But they would always have that bond of friendship.

"Wondering if you would care to meet me in your little town for dinner?" he asked. "I'm dying to come out to your dig, but Sterling warned me off. A simple, 'where's Tallie?' landed me in the principal's office. So now I'm more curious than ever."

Tallie laughed. "I would love to. I've been thinking about a trip into town anyway."

"How about seven?"

"Perfect. I've been told there's a little family-run diner that has great food. Everything from sandwiches to steaks. It's called Frieda's Sandwich Shoppe. Apparently there is more on the menu than the name would imply."

"Sounds great. I'll see you then."

Tallie realized her stomach was much better today

and she was hungry. That was happening more and more often. She assumed it was because of the pregnancy. There was no sign of Cole. He must have been detained in Houston. She would drive into town and meet Stan for dinner. A steak sounded good. And a piece of coconut pie. Maybe Frieda had that on the menu, as well.

When Cole arrived at the old cabin, Tallie was nowhere to be found. Only after checking the river and the dig areas did he realize her Ford wagon was missing. Apparently she'd had enough of the heat, the bugs and the rodents. How long would she be away? Cole felt a sinking feeling. Where had she gone?

It would have been nice if she had told him or someone on the ranch that she was leaving. The idea of her disappearing didn't sit well. He'd become used to her being here every day. He'd driven here with the intention of asking her to come to the house for the night.

On his way back to the estate his cell phone began to ring.

"Hey, little brother." Wade's voice came over the phone.

"Hey, man. Haven't talked with you in almost a month. How was the trip? Or are you still in London?" Wade had been negotiating the acquisition of a boutique hotel chain to expand Masters Corporation's presence in Europe.

"Nope. Got home last night," Wade explained.

"There have been some changes. Thought you might like to have an update and I need your signature on a couple of documents."

"How about steaks and a couple of cold ones at Frieda's?"

"Done. Give me an hour and I'll be there."

When Cole got to town an hour later, the small eatery was packed. Not surprising for Frieda's on a Saturday night. Cole spotted Wade at a table along the wall and headed in that direction. The diner was a laid-back kind of place but served the best food in three counties. After each of them gave their order Wade asked, "So, how's it going with your archeologist? Have you been able to reclaim the land where Tallie is digging and move forward with construction?"

Cole shook his head. "No. Tallie is going to be here for a while. I've done all I dare do to *entice* her to leave. I'm just going to let it play out. She had Tom Mitchell call me."

"I was there the day he called, remember?" The grin on Wade's face said he was not above teasing Cole about the entire ordeal, somewhere Cole didn't want to go. Circumstances had changed but he didn't intend to enlighten Wade tonight.

"I don't think it's that damn funny."

"Do you honestly think she doesn't know who was behind all the shenanigans?"

"She does. But she is as good at giving back as she is at taking."

"Really?" Wade tilted his head for a harder look

at his brother. "I've always wanted to meet the girl who brought Cole Masters to his knees." He chuckled again. "She must be one hell of a woman minus the mud pack."

Before Cole could answer, the small bell above the door tinkled, indicating a new customer had entered the diner.

"You're about to get your chance to find out."

Cole watched his brother turn and gaze at the sexy woman who'd just come in, her long black hair swinging against her shoulders and down past her waist. She responded to the wave from a man at a table not far away. A man several years her senior.

"Brother—" Wade leaned toward Cole "—I'd have to say you have a bigger problem than putting up with an archeology dig. Damn. She is hot. I'll trade places with you anytime. Just say the word."

"I don't think there is a word," Cole responded, suddenly overwhelmed with a protective instinct. He wasn't sure what brought it on or what triggered it but his love-'em-and-leave-'em brother could stay the hell away from Tallie. And another quick glance at Tallie with the older man clearly showed they had a close rapport. Dr. Tallie Finley might be taken, anyway. And didn't that set well? Small wonder she didn't want to stay at Cole's house.

Tallie immediately spotted Stan as he waved to her from a table. When she drew closer she was surprised to see David Sloan sitting with him. They were all employees of the museum and all great friends. After hugs all around, they sat and barely stopped talking long enough to look at a menu. After ordering, the two men wanted to know the focus of her dig—why she was here.

"Sterling is tight-lipped," Stan said. "We didn't think he was even going to tell us where you were. So, what's the deal?"

"There isn't one," Tallie replied. Seeing the skepticism on their faces she added, "There really isn't. When my grandmother died she left me a map, supposedly marking the spot of the original village of our ancestors, and asked me to see if I could find it." She shrugged. "So that's what I'm doing. I had some leave time before the Brazil trip so Sterling said if I wanted to do this…do it."

"And here I was imagining the find of the decade and getting jealous as hell," Stan admitted and everyone laughed.

"Dr. Sterling did say something about your host, the guy who owns the land. Is he really that bad or is Sterling making mountains out of molehills again?"

"He really is that bad," came a deep voice from behind Tallie. "I can guarantee it. Wouldn't you agree, Dr. Finley?"

Tallie tensed as she realized Cole Masters was standing directly behind her. Her dinner partners' eyes were focused above her head; their mouths hung open. She turned partially around in her seat so she could answer him.

"Absolutely. Without any doubt whatsoever he is,

by far, the worst landowner I've ever had the bad luck to work with." She forced a broad smile.

"See, I told you," he addressed the group.

"Cole, these are my friends and coworkers, Doctors Stan Bridger and David Sloan."

"And, like Dr. Finley, both of you dig up bones for a living?"

His eyes sparkled. He was so handsome, so charming. He would undoubtedly have her associates eating out of his hand in no time.

"We confess." Stan laughed. "Would you care to join us?"

Had Stan just invited him to sit at their table? She didn't want Cole sitting with them. He wouldn't understand half of their dialogue and she, at least, wouldn't understand his. They were so different. He dealt with blueprints and erecting skyscrapers; she with old maps and digging up the past. She felt the warmth of his large hands on her shoulders as though he was ensuring his claim was known by all. She might be carrying his child but that didn't mean she had become his property.

"Thank you, but I'm here with my brother. We have some business to discuss. Maybe another time?"

Tallie looked to her left toward the table where Wade was sitting. Their gazes met and he smiled and nodded.

Wade stood and made his way over to their table. Cole seemed surprised but made the introductions. Wade seemed keen on holding Tallie's hand far longer than the norm. She couldn't miss the sparkle of interest in his eyes.

"I hope all of you have a nice dinner," Cole said, stepping between Tallie and his brother. "I can vouch for Frieda. Everything on the menu is delicious. It was good to meet you all."

"You, as well," Stan and David chimed in.

Cole and Wade returned to their seats just as a waitress set their plates on the table.

"Don't say it," Cole warned his brother.

"Say what?" Wade asked, total innocence on his face.

"I know you're about to say something crude having to do with my relationship with Dr. Finley. She is just an archeologist doing some work on land I happen to own."

Wade finished chewing and wiped his mouth. "I was merely going to suggest you put it in a higher gear before someone beats you to it. The way you looked at her? The way she looked at you? I know how much you were hurt by Gina. But that was over three years ago. If you let this one get away, you're an idiot."

"Well, thanks for sharing your thoughts."

"Hey, any time, brother."

Eleven

Cole continued to watch Wade with a knowing eye. Often Wade's glance would trail back to Tallie, but he never said another word about her, which was the norm for Wade. He would speak his mind once then drop the subject. The problem was that Cole saw the same thing. He felt what Wade described. The one thing he was dead wrong about was assuming three years was long enough to get over what had happened with Gina and the baby she'd carried.

The emotions that ran through Cole were strong, deep and confusing. His wife had been pregnant with another man's child yet had vowed that she loved Cole. She'd sworn her love to him while all the time she'd pledged that same love to someone else. That was if the woman could love at all. If there was even such a thing as love. If Cole had it to do over, knowing what he knew now, he'd just give her whatever she wanted. Then, perhaps, he wouldn't have ordered her from the house and she wouldn't have driven so recklessly that she went over the cliff, killing her and her baby. But she had played him. And he'd sworn he would never be caught with his pants down again. He wouldn't be the idiot twice.

He'd assumed what he felt for Gina in the beginning was love. But the bitterness that rose within him at her treachery trumped any other feeling. He didn't know, would never know, what love was or if there really was such a thing. The entire concept was dubious, at best, and eventually he'd grown weary of trying to make sense of it. If he needed a woman, he'd find a willing one and that would be the end of it. Never again would he be made such a fool.

He looked toward Tallie. She was talking and laughing with her friends. It hit him hard: this was the first time he had really seen her laugh and show true happiness. A sickening knot grew in his throat as he remembered all the mean pranks he'd thrown her way. Any one of them could have caused her to be hurt in some way. From now on he would do anything necessary to ensure her safety. And that included getting her to move into the house and out of that shack.

"So, what's your schedule like?" Cole asked his brother. Anything to distract himself from thinking Tallie might be a crook in archeologist's clothing.

"I have a full day tomorrow, meetings back-to-back, then a return to Paris for the meeting with Yves Bordeaux." Wade laid his napkin next to his empty plate. "I'm afraid I'm gonna have to cut out on you early."

"I understand. Before you leave…has there been any news on Dad's will?"

"Not a word. Apparently it's more involved than we thought." Wade shrugged. "Valuing a company whose holdings continue to change and grow daily will be a challenge. I don't envy the team of attorneys and CPAs whose task it is to figure it all out."

"I agree. I only mentioned it because I don't like something hanging over my head. Dad acted so different the last few years of his life. There are several deals hinging on what's in that will. It's been months. People are starting to call. I'd just like to get it off my plate."

"I'm with you, bro. That thought has run through my head more than once."

"I'll call the attorneys tomorrow. Whatever Dad decided in the will, all we can do is agree with it or contest it, but it's past time we got to it."

They finished up the business and Wade got Cole's signature on some legal papers. Then, with a handshake-turned-man-hug and a quick slap on the back, Wade made his way to a waiting car that would return him to the county helipad where he would fly back to Dallas.

Cole took one last look at Tallie before he followed his brother out the door into the warm night air. In the parking lot he sat in his car, his finger

poised over the start button. About then Tallie and
her friends walked around the corner of the building. The younger man hugged her goodbye and got
in his small car and drove off. Tallie slipped inside
her old Ford wagon and the older man got into his
vehicle. He turned his car toward the exit. Tallie followed. Both turned right.

Where were they going? The route to the ranch
was in the opposite direction. His hands on the steering wheel and foot on the gas seemed to take over
as he pulled his car out behind them. Regardless of
telling himself no, that he had no right to do this,
he kept going.

Within three blocks the first car turned into the
parking lot of a small motel and she drove in behind
him. Cole had his answer. He drove past in time to
see Tallie walk toward one of the rooms. His hands
clenched the steering wheel while his jaw muscles
worked overtime.

At the next light, he made a U-turn and headed
back to the ranch.

When he got home, he closed the door and tossed
his keys on the kitchen counter then made his way
to the bar and poured two fingers of Crown Royal
before flopping down onto the overstuffed leather
sofa. The window gave him a distant view of the
acres he'd purchased adjacent to the family ranch
for the purpose of building the lodge and cabins for
the corporate retreat project. Usually somewhere
out in the darkness he could see a small glow from

Tallie's barrage of candles she'd begun to leave lit while she'd slept. There were no lights on tonight.

Cole finished the drink and headed to the bar for another. Enough of these and he wouldn't give Tallie another thought. *Maybe. Nah.* With no conscious decision he opened the French door and stepped out into the evening shadows. Still no sign of any light from the shack. Was she still at the motel? He huffed out a sigh. *Let it go.* She'd most likely be there all night. Feeling anxious, he decided to make a quick drive over just to make sure everything was as it should be.

He pulled out his cell phone, called her number and listened to the ringing on the line.

"Hello?"

It was the deeper voice of a man.

"Sorry," Cole said. "I must have the wrong number."

"Are you calling for Tallie?"

"Yes."

"You've got the right number. She's stepped away for a few minutes but she'll be right back. Would you like to hold or leave a message?"

The man's voice sounded tired, sluggish. Cole had to wonder what the guy had been doing to make him sound so fatigued. *Not your business.*

"No," Cole replied. "This is Cole Masters. I had a question for her but it will wait until tomorrow."

"I'll let her know you called."

Cole terminated the call. So, the good doctor had a man in her life. Good for her. He had to admit he was surprised, but why should he be? She was an incredibly beautiful woman. She probably had men lining up around the block.

Cole felt a sinking sensation in the pit of his stomach. This time he knew exactly why. He wanted her. In his mind he saw her lying back in his bed, those green eyes welcoming, calling him to come to her. He knew how she tasted and he wanted more. He wanted to again run his hands over her silken skin; he wanted to feel the heat from her body. Feel her quiver in anticipation. Anything she wanted of him, he would give her.

Damn. He had to stop this. She was obviously involved with someone. Even if she wasn't, their time together hadn't exactly been a whirlwind of friendship and, in a matter of weeks, she would be gone. But the governor was right. Cole needed to take care of her: see that she slept in safe, cool surroundings and had appropriate food and water. He could also try harder to find someone to help her. First thing in the morning he would put the idea into motion.

Whether she liked it or not.

He heard the ringtone on his phone. It was Tallie. "Hey."

"Stan said you called. Is everything all right?"

"I just wanted to make sure you were planning on sleeping at the house tonight."

"Oh." She sounded hesitant. If she was coming from another man's bed, how could he expect her to sound any other way? He swallowed back the bile that rose in his throat at the thought of another man touching her, making love to her.

"Tallie, I won't allow you to live in that shack one more minute. It isn't good for you."

"We can talk about that when I get back. Now, if there isn't anything else…?"

"No. Nothing else."

She ended the call and his anger surged. Maybe he had been a bit overbearing but she had to see it was out of concern. He glanced at the lighted dial of his watch. Ten o'clock. Why not just wait for her at the old cabin? He was sure she wouldn't come back to the house. And he knew that if he stayed there and waited for her, he'd have a restless night.

Two hours later there was still no sign of Tallie. Was she really going to spend the night with that man? A red glaze of anger obscured Cole's vision and, with no further thought, he got into his pickup and headed to town. He drove straight to the little motel, walked up to the room he'd seen her enter and beat on the door.

Finally, after another round of knocking, the man opened the door. He'd obviously been asleep.

"Where is Tallie?" Cole almost barked.

The man looked confused. "She went home. Rather, she went back to her dig."

"I just came from there. Her vehicle isn't there and neither is she. When did she leave here?"

"Right after she talked with you. She was upset."

"She isn't the only one." Cole glanced at the bed. There was no indication that two people were sharing it. The unused pillow was still draped in the cheap bedcover.

"Look, man," Stan said. "She was just here going over some pics on my laptop of my latest dig. If you feel this way about her, you really should be up front. Tell her. She was hurt once. The guy went as far as to ask her to marry him then disappeared when some woman he thought was better came along. Not even a note. Nothing. Personally, I don't think you can find a better woman and, if my wife wouldn't get all bent out of shape, I might pursue Tallie myself. Now, is there anything else?"

Cole muttered an apology for disturbing the man and returned to his truck. When he arrived home, he entered through the back door and trudged up the stairs to his room, shedding his knit shirt as he went. Out of curiosity, he opened the door to the bedroom he'd given Tallie the night she'd been sick. Sure enough a small glow from the lights outside showed a sleeping form. He flipped on the overhead light.

"Oh! Turn off that light," she whispered and pulled a pillow over her eyes. "Where have you been?"

"Out looking for you."

At that she pushed the pillow away and rolled toward him. "Why? Did I misunderstand your *demand*?"

"No, you didn't. You're in exactly the right place."

"Then turn off the light and leave me alone."

Cole ran his hand over his face. The entire time he'd waited for her by the shack, she had been in his house asleep. He didn't know whether to laugh or cry. He flipped off the light and moved toward her bed, sitting on the edge.

"Tallie."

"Hmm?"

"Are you and your friend in a serious relationship?"

The minutes passed until he thought she wasn't going to answer. She sat up and twisted around until she could see his face. "You mean Stan?"

"Yeah." Cole nodded.

"I told you, Stan is an old friend." She glared at him. "He is also married with three kids. You must not think very much of me at all to ask me that. It's discomforting you think most of what I say is a lie."

"Most people lie."

"Well, I'm not one of them," she snapped.

Cole didn't know what to say. Once again he'd put his foot squarely in his mouth.

Tallie threw aside the covers. "I'm going back to the cabin. I should not have come here in the first place."

"Tallie."

"First you strong-arm me into coming here, which I only did because you were right about getting out of the heat. But I am not about to stay with a man who thinks of me that way. You are an arrogant snob. So disappointing." She slid out of the bed and went to the bedroom closet to pull out a pair of jeans and a shirt. "And don't you dare try and boss me around again."

In a heartbeat Cole sprang from the bed and beat her to the closet door. Tallie looked up into his eyes and he saw the glimmer of passion in her emerald depths. Without waiting for permission, he scooped her into his arms and carried her to his bed.

"What are you doing?" she asked. "Put me down."

He set her on her feet but rather than turn away, he slowly began to unbutton the tiny buttons of her nightshirt. When it fell to the floor he removed her panties and she was standing naked in front of him, the memory of a beautiful vision coming true. Her curves were more luscious than ever; roughing it in the trapper's cabin had had no impact whatsoever on her incredible figure.

His erection was straining almost painfully against his jeans. Before he could release himself, Tallie was there, her hands unsnapping then lowering the zipper. Without saying a word she pushed his pants over his hips, freeing his erection.

Cole kicked off his jeans, picked her up and placed her on the bed.

Pushing her back on the bed Cole was once again enthralled as the taste and the scent of her surrounded him. His mouth came down over hers as his larger body molded to her. She was his. He wanted to brand her so that no other man would ever touch her this way.

Tallie writhed beneath him. He remembered how she moved, how she whimpered with need, and how those light, feminine sounds made him fight to keep his control. How she sent him whirling like no other woman he'd ever bedded. He kissed her neck, nibbling on her ear before going farther down her body. Her breasts were ripe and when his mouth closed on a swollen rosy tip, her hands grabbed his hair and held him to her. She arched her back, her breasts swelling beneath his touch.

He rose and with one hand positioned himself at her core She was hot and moist. He pushed in gently, savoring the feel of her. Her breathing intensified. Then as his body began to move, he had no clear thoughts of anything or anyone but Tallie.

The passion between them grew until he felt his body quiver with the need for release. He knew she was close by the way she responded. He pulled out and kissed her belly then farther down. Tallie grew still then cried out as she climaxed. Cole held her until she calmed.

He reentered her and as he pushed in deep he knew he couldn't hold out much longer. He brought her to the peak once again and felt the tingling sensation in his lower back telling him there was no turning back. This time when Tallie climaxed, Cole was right there with her. Then he kissed her gently, pulled the covers over them and held her close.

Tallie loved making love with Cole. She loved being with him even though at times he was overbearing and demanding, always wanting his way. So far, his intentions had been good, but the reality was that she would soon be several months along and someone like Cole Masters didn't appear in public with a pregnant woman at his side. It would ruin his playboy image and the tabloids would go crazy. And, honestly, it was more than she wanted to put herself through.

Cole was devoted to his business, as she was to her job. Both required them to be gone for months at a time. He lived in a world of money and privilege. Hers was a quiet life of digging in the dirt. She couldn't think of one single thing they had in common other than the baby he didn't know about. According to the internet articles she'd read about him, he was a man who hadn't changed his lifestyle in all of his adult life. But having a baby with Tallie would be a big change. For him and for her.

He would have to deal with a stubborn woman who would not listen or follow his demands. She did not do demands. He would have to realize when she'd had enough and know when to back off. She was independent while Cole was overprotective. It was a hopeless situation. Her mind kept silently screaming for him to just leave her alone. Her heart said to take what he was offering and just love him. But how much would he love her when he found out about the baby?

Tallie felt like a rug had just been pulled out from under her. Hopefully she could find proof of her family's beginnings and leave before Cole was ever the wiser.

Twelve

When he'd made love to her last night, it was like their shared night in the Big Easy on steroids. The passion was just as hot as it had been the first time only without the fear involved in opening herself to a complete stranger. He was so strong and, she had to admit, there were times when she didn't mind his demands so much.

Why couldn't he have been a normal guy? One who drank beer instead of imported hundred-year-old whiskey? A guy who liked to watch sports on TV with his buddies instead of from a box on the fifty-yard line? A man who drove his car to work every day, not one who got in one of three helicopters and flew away. He was a billionaire. And Tallie didn't know how to relate to such a person. Or even if she wanted to.

If she could view him as normal, there were a hundred-plus things to love about him. But the hard fact was that he was not a regular guy and never would be. The ego, the arrogance, the expectations, the demands. Life was too short to put up with that. She'd lived through eight long months with John, who'd had the same qualities, and she'd ended up being dumped, her heart and her pride shattered. No way would she put herself in that situation again, especially with Cole. She knew if she ever let her barriers down, the love she had for Cole would be so much deeper, more profound. And if he walked away she might never recover.

Tallie dressed and went downstairs. There was no sign of Cole. She followed her nose to the kitchen where the tea was brewing.

"If you need Mr. Cole," said Martha, the kind maid who worked with Chef Andre in the kitchen, "he said he was going to the main barn."

"Thank you."

Tallie could swing by there on her way to the dig. Grabbing a hot cup of tea, she stepped outside. She passed through the back gate of the estate grounds and followed the natural-stone footpath to the large, sprawling building.

She heard neighing from inside the barn and her pace quickened. She loved horses. She'd had one in her younger years but had had to sell her when she'd left for college. Now, being here on the ranch, she missed that mare more than ever.

Midway down the main aisle Cole stood talking with another man holding a baby. She didn't want to interrupt so she slipped past them and continued down the wide stable aisle, looking at the horses in their stalls. Magnificent was the word that came to mind. Their sleek, shiny coats gleamed under the barn lights. Ears alert, they nickered to her as she passed.

"Tallie," Cole called to her. "Come back. There's someone I want you to meet."

He reached out for her when she got close and pulled her against him, his arm going around her shoulders.

"Tallie, this is my brother, Chance. Chance, meet Dr. Finley."

"Very nice to meet you." He extended his hand.

"You, as well."

"And this young lady in my arms is Emma. She's my wife's niece but we're raising her as our own daughter."

The child was adorable. "Hi, Emma."

"Momie gonna wide hawsee. Daddy say no but Momie not yisen."

"Where did the two of you meet?" Chance asked, switching Emma to his other arm.

"New Orleans," Cole answered. "A little over five months ago."

"That long, huh?" Chance grinned. "That's encouraging."

"When you find what you've been searching for, why waste time?"

Tallie stood there in complete shock. Cole was lying to his brother. Yes, they had met in New Orleans, but everything after that was a trumped-up story. Cole Masters could have any woman he wanted. He certainly hadn't been searching for *her*. In that moment she wished things between them could be different: that Cole was really in love with her and wanted to marry her just because she was who she was. But Cinderella dreams were not in abundance this year.

"Cole!" called a young woman leading a large, dapple-gray thoroughbred toward them. She was beautiful, with angelic features and long, silver-blond hair. Without pausing she stepped into Cole's arms. "Even when you stay here on the ranch I never get to see you."

"I guess today is your lucky day."

"In your dreams."

"Holly, this is Dr. Tallie Finley," Cole said. "She's an archeologist doing some excavating on that land I purchased a few years ago."

Holly turned toward her, a wide grin on her face. "Very nice to meet you."

"Tallie, this is Dr. Holly Masters, Chance's wife."

"Who's going to put that horse right back inside his stall," Chance stated firmly, which caused Holly to roll her eyes.

"I don't know how long you'll be here," Holly said to Tallie, "but one thing you'll soon learn about the

Masters brothers is they are all bossy control freaks. Always have been, now that I think about it."

She turned to her husband. "I'm just going for a short ride, *dear.*"

Chance pulled his wife to him and kissed her. "We just found out Holly is pregnant. The doctor said no horses until after the baby is born. Some hardheaded mothers-to-be just refuse to listen to common sense."

"Congratulations," Tallie said. "To both of you. That's wonderful."

"We gonna has baby," Emma chimed in.

"We just moved into our new house on the ranch. If you can spare the time, come over and visit for a while."

"I would like that. Thank you." Tallie was moved by the kind invitation.

Cole took her hand, said his goodbyes and walked with Tallie out of the barn toward the house.

"It was nice meeting your brothers. You have a great family."

"You sound surprised."

"No, not at all."

"It was good to see Chance. The three of us rarely get together anymore. As Holly said, they just finished building their home about five miles away from the original house, the one Dad built for Mom, which is where I've been staying. Chance was in the SEALs but while he was home on leave after an injury he started seeing Holly and he never signed up for another tour. Instead he took over running the

Circle M. When the profits began to soar, no one was surprised."

"What about Wade? Does he live here, as well?"

"Wade lives in the family mansion in Dallas. It's close to the airport and built for entertaining and meetings. Since Wade does most of the traveling and entertaining, it works out well."

"And what about you?"

He shrugged. "I live here and there, wherever I'm needed at the time."

"So you were telling the truth that night in New Orleans."

He laughed. "Yeah. For the most part. But I can honestly say I've never spent a night under a bridge."

"You did look like a bum."

"That wasn't exactly the plan, but it had a good outcome, don't you think?"

"I have to go this way," she said, turning away and purposely not answering his question.

"Tallie, why don't you let someone else look for the artifacts?"

She shook her head. "I could use the help. I won't deny that. But it's my dig, Cole. I promised my grandmother I would find the proof that an ancient tribe lived in this area. It's my responsibility. I intend to shorten my work days and not be out in the heat so long. I'll be careful, but I must try and find…what I'm searching for." Whatever that turned out to be.

She could tell Cole wanted to argue with her; she felt his body tighten. But he said nothing and for that she was grateful.

"Then I'll see you later."

"Absolutely."

A week later Tallie had barely finished her morning tea, which she still took outside the trapper's cabin even though she was now living under Cole's roof, when a strange car rolled up to the site. The doors opened and four young women got out of the vehicle; the driver remained at the wheel. They all walked toward Tallie, excitement on their faces. Before Tallie could ask who they were and why there were there, Cole's pickup pulled up next to the car. He got out, grinning from ear to ear. Yep. Whatever this was, Cole Masters was behind it.

Their eyes met and his sparkled with mischief.

"Good morning, Dr. Finley," he said as he nodded to the four women. "Have you met them yet?"

Tallie shook her head. "No."

"Carolyn Hicks, Amy Knell, April Hastings and Kathy Brown. These exceptional students all have a perfect grade-point average and are majoring in anthropology or archeology at area universities."

Cole had a smile that reminded her of the fat cat that ate the canary.

"They all applied for internships at various museums for the summer. All were turned down because of budget restraints. I managed to correct that small issue and here they are. Ready to go to work. They are actually excited to help you dig in the dirt. Go figure."

He turned to the four students. "This is Dr. Finley. She is the one you will be helping."

Tallie was speechless. "Do...do any of you have any experience?"

All but one raised their hands. The one who apparently didn't have experience looked anxious.

"Well, if you have an idea of what this is about and can dig carefully, I can teach you the rest. Welcome. And thank you all. I really do need your help.

"Look in the back of my old wagon and you will find a box with extra hand tools and brushes. Get a small hand shovel, a four-inch rake and two brushes—one small, one large. The site is that way. If you grab your supplies and head over toward that sifter, I'll be with you in just a few minutes. Did everyone bring water bottles?"

They all nodded; two of the women held theirs up.

"Good. Hop to it."

"I can't believe you did this." Tallie turned to Cole.

"What? You don't want them?"

"No. Yes! They'll be great. I was about the same age when I was selected for my first dig. It will give them valuable experience and help me, as well. Thank you, Cole." And without thinking she bounded into his arms and hugged him tight. "Thank you so much."

She felt his arms go around her back and squeeze her gently to him. Then his arms dropped and she stepped back.

"You're welcome." She couldn't miss the twinkle

in those hazel eyes. He handed her a manila envelope. "Inside is the basic information on each student and their signed wavers. I'll provide a place for them to stay and all the meals."

For the first time in what felt like forever, Tallie was speechless.

"Tallie?"

"Why are you doing this?"

"Let's just say I want my field back."

"But all of this trouble…it must be costing a fortune."

"It's really not that much. I want to do it, Tallie. I look at it as a donation. Find your artifacts. I want to see your face when you show me the first one." He must have seen her look of astonishment because he made no attempt to hide his grin. "I'll catch you tonight."

Tallie stood in the shade of the giant oak tree and watched until he drove out of sight. If she was dreaming, she never wanted to wake up.

The girls proved every bit as knowledgeable and eager as she'd first surmised. She gathered them in a small circle and explained what they were looking for. She couldn't tell them they were looking for a new civilization, but did confirm they were searching for artifacts from a tribe that dated back several thousand years.

"Beads, pieces of jewelry, pots in part or whole," she told them. "Keep an eye open for anything that looks like it could be made by man. Also, you might happen on petrified seeds, plants or bulbs. There are two grids. Two of you take one, the other two take the second. If you find anything you can't identify, set it to one side for me to look at. Do you have any questions?"

Once all the questions were asked and answered, Tallie left them and walked closer to the cliff. Through her binoculars, she again searched for any sign of caves or openings between the massive rocks and boulders. The same dark, shadowy area she'd spotted last week still called to her. It might be worth the effort to climb up and check it out from a closer viewpoint. But in her condition, she didn't know how a climb like that would be possible.

With stakes and string she outlined a third grid and got to work. The hours flew by. It was almost two o'clock when she heard a strange honk and looked in the direction from which it came. It was a bus. No. An RV. Followed by a car. The massive recreational vehicle came to a stop just to the other side of the old trapper's cabin. The sight brought Tallie to her feet. Cole had said he was going to provide lodging for the students. And here it was.

"Hey, guys," she called to the college students, "I've gotta return to the cabin for just a few minutes. I'll be back as soon as I can. Take a break and make sure you stay hydrated!"

Dropping her tools, she jogged in the direction of the RV. The driver, a robust man in his fifties, was just stepping out when she reached the door.

"Good afternoon," he said. "Are you Dr. Finley?"

"Yes."

"I'm Clay with Big D RVs out of Dallas. If you wouldn't mind, I need you to check the RV inside and out. If you find everything is okay, I'll ask you to sign that you received the vehicle and all is in order. First let me get it set up. Is the location okay or do you want it moved?"

"It's perfect where it is."

"Good. There is some leveling we need to do and it has four extensions, plus the main compartment will about double in size. Let me get the TV and all the extras set up then I'll need you to give it a look."

When he was done preparing the RV, Tallie stepped into the amazing vehicle.

Clay adjusted his cap, scratched his chin and gazed longingly at the river. "Any fish in that stream?"

"I think there might be, yes. You're welcome to see for yourself."

"Good. While you do the inspection, I think I might have a look."

The RV was enormous. She had no idea a recreational vehicle could be so luxurious. There was a master bedroom plus two smaller ones, a whirlpool tub, even two, big, flat-screen TVs with satellite, one in the master bedroom and a larger one in the living area. The entire vehicle was actually larger than her apartment. The air-conditioning was pure heaven. It contained state-of-the-art appliances, granite countertops, even a small chandelier in the main living area. And the kitchen was fully stocked.

As she stepped outside another car drove up and

a man got out holding several large boxes of pizza and a case of sodas. "Dr. Finley?"

"That would be me."

"I've got your lunch. Where would you like me to put it?"

Tallie knew Cole was behind all this. He had said he would provide a place for the students to stay and all meals were on him. "Put them over on the porch of the old cabin for now."

"Yes, ma'am," he said and walked in that direction.

Jogging down the hill, she gathered the students and told them about the pizzas and soft drinks. That seemed to lighten their mood even more.

They all gathered on the rickety porch and didn't hesitate to open the boxes and grab ice-cold cans of soda.

"When you've finished eating, you are welcome to go inside the RV and check out your new home." They all looked long and hard at it. First one then all headed in that direction, forgetting about the food.

Cole Masters was a take-charge kind of guy. If she accepted this, what was next? Her heart missed a beat at the thought.

After signing the inspection papers, Tallie drove to the mansion. Finding the door unlocked, she stepped inside and closed it behind her. She stood in front of his office door, waiting for him to finish his phone call, ignoring his gestures to come farther into the room. Finally he ended the call and stood, an unmistakable mischievous light shining in his soft brown eyes.

"The RV was just delivered," she said, wrapping her arms around her chest, suddenly a bit uncomfortable. "Thank you."

"You're welcome. The girls can move in there for the duration of the dig.

"I intend to donate it to your museum after you leave. They can use it or sell it. I don't care. But I do care about your safety."

"But—"

"No buts. The RV is for the students. A guard will be on duty at all times during the evening hours. We don't have any crime to speak of around here but I will feel better if someone is out there making sure it stays that way. You can continue to stay here. You need rest, which it's doubtful you'll get if you try living with those college kids. They'll probably keep you up until four every morning."

There was a moment when neither Tallie nor Cole moved. Tallie was held by the strength of his gaze; she was close enough to see the different colors of gold and brown in his eyes. There was even a touch of green.

Almost in slow motion he dipped his head and kissed her.

She heard him draw in a deep breath as his hand cupped the back of her head, his fingers threading through her hair. Feeling her response, he quickly took the kiss up to the level of a sensual demand. She was lost. The scent of his cologne surrounded her, his strong arms held her firmly against him. But she wasn't going anywhere. His hungry mouth feasted on hers, his tongue seeking hidden places. Absently her hands clutched his shirt, pulling him nearer even though there was only one way they could get any closer. That thought propelled her out of his arms, breaking their amazing kiss.

To become involved with Cole would be to commit emotional suicide. Her heart would become involved and it was almost guaranteed he would then tire of her and disappear.

"I can't do this," she whispered against his lips. "I need to get back to the dig."

She turned and headed for the door.

"Tallie, wait," Cole called to her.

But Tallie didn't stop or slow down. As tempting as he was, she couldn't let herself be swayed into a brief affair regardless of how badly her body wanted him. The effect of his kiss was still raging through her body, the need for him pooling deep in her belly. But she would not be a fool again.

By the time she'd returned to the dig she was in more control. Her mind had cleared enough that she had regained her focus. She had to do more, work harder and faster, so she could leave. Before she had to tell him about the baby and bear his wrath.

By four o'clock she called a halt to the day. The temperature was in the nineties. Everyone needed a break, including her. She had twice stepped on tree stubs, leaving the bottom of her left foot bruised. It hurt like the dickens.

Tallie gathered her backpack from the cabin and headed for the main house on the hill. In a few minutes she had her soiled clothes washing, found a box of crackers and a jar of peanut butter in the kitchen and fixed a glass of iced tea. As bad as she wanted a shower, she made it no further than the large bedroom upstairs. Setting her glass, the crackers and peanut butter on the nightstand, she pulled back the covers and fell into bed. Sleep wasted no time in claiming her.

Thirteen

Tallie woke sometime in the night. A night-light provided just enough glow that she could see and recognize the furniture and doorway leading into the huge en suite bathroom. Throwing back the covers, she walked toward the bathroom. She wanted to get into that huge tub and let the jets massage her from every direction. It would feel amazing.

She turned on the water and heard a soft knock on the bedroom door. She went and opened it. It was Cole.

"I saw the light under the door. Are you all right? Is there anything you need?"

"Nope." She turned toward the bathroom. "I'm good. Just woke up and wanted a bath." She began to remove her T-shirt...and stopped. Cole was still standing in the room. When she stopped, it took him a second to realize he needed to leave.

"Could I borrow another T-shirt? I need to do laundry."

"Sure."

She wouldn't admit it out loud but she preferred staying here versus staying in the RV with four excited, talkative college students. While she was plenty thankful for their assistance, she preferred some peace and quiet.

When she got in the tub, she quickly applied body wash and felt the silken suds roll down her body. She began to wash her hair in the same wonderful herbal solution as the body wash.

When she was done, she grabbed a towel and quickly dried herself off. It was then she again heard a soft knock on the bedroom door. Encircling her body with the towel, she answered the knock. Cole stood there with a couple of navy blue T-shirts.

"Oh, thank you." She reached out to take them. As soon as she did, the towel slipped. Grabbing for it did no good. She looked up at Cole.

He reminded her of a golden warrior with his tanned skin and sun-bleached hair. His shirt hung open, partially revealing a muscled chest and ripped abs. Slowly she lowered her hands, no longer caring that she was naked or that Cole was standing two feet in front of her. She felt his hot gaze roam over her breasts and her nipples hardened under his gaze.

Cole stood in front of her, letting her see the smoldering desire in his eyes. His erection signified that she wasn't alone in her need. He was a handsome man, a brilliant man. Forget about the money. That night in the French Quarter had been a turning point for Tallie. Cole had showed her how glorious sex with the right man could be.

She went to step back but before she did Cole came forward. Not one word was spoken as he gently cupped the back of her neck and slowly pulled her to him. With a deep groan, he plunged his tongue inside her mouth. Cole enticed her to open her mouth wider as though he was willing to fill it with all she needed.

With an almost savage moan, he cupped her face in his hands and he went deeper, searching the hidden depths of her mouth, taking his time as though this was a moment that had to last a lifetime. He tasted of wine and mint. But it was the scorching heat that told her exactly what he wanted. He changed his stance, moving still closer, and his big hands cupped her hips, pulling her hard against his obvious desire. He was grinding against her, making the fire pool in her lower regions.

Suddenly he spun her around and pushed her up against a wall, his body holding her in place. He moaned as he kissed her even more deeply. His hard, muscular body pushed against her, hips moving, letting her feel his erection before taking it away. Tallie couldn't suppress the frustrated groan. She grabbed hold of his shirt and tried to pull him to her. He huffed a laugh and tore the shirt off. Tallie began to unbuckle his belt.

* * *

Cole hadn't meant to hover in the doorway while bringing the T-shirt to Tallie. He'd been so overwhelmed by her beauty he couldn't have turned and left had his life depended on it. Again, he couldn't help noticing how voluptuous she looked. It was like watching nature in its purest, most beautiful form. On her face was surprise. In her mesmerizing green eyes, honest desire. He had grabbed on to that need and refused to let go unless she said one word: no.

There were at least a hundred reasons why he should have walked away and only one why he didn't: he'd never wanted a woman so badly in his life.

Her body was hot from the warmth of the water, her skin smooth as the finest silk. She tasted like the wild berries that grew deep in the vistas near the towering pine and oak trees. When he drew back to look at her lovely face, he swallowed hard. Unbridled passion surged through him, his erection straining against his jeans until it was painful. Her eyes were closed, her head was tilted back, her mouth open, lips pink and swollen from his kiss. She grasped his shoulders as he traced a line of heat down her throat to the junction of her shoulder with his tongue. He nipped at the velvety skin and thought he would die of pleasure.

Her hands had stilled on his belt, the passion of their embrace apparently taking her mind down a different path. He quickly unbuckled the buckle and unzipped his jeans, pushing them down just enough.

His hands roamed over her back and down past the waist to her hips. He didn't pause before he lifted her and settled her body against him, entering her slowly, watching for any signs of discomfort. She moaned and lifted her legs to go around his hips; her head fell back against the wall and she moaned in ecstasy.

"I can't go slow," he said as he felt his control slipping.

"Then don't," she whispered.

He entered her body fully, completely, with one hard thrust. Tallie whimpered and, gripping his shoulders, pulled his head to hers for another kiss. Cole did not disappoint. The feel of her holding him was unlike anything he'd ever experienced. So tight.

His body began to move, pulling out, entering again. Over and over; again and again. Suddenly she threw her head back, her climax fully overtaking her. It almost took him with her, but he held on, wanting to give her more pleasure. He wasn't nearly finished with this incredible woman who had come into his life so unexpectedly.

With her legs still wrapped around his waist, he carried her to the bed, laying her down on the silken coverlet, never breaking the link between them.

"Tallie," he whispered softly.

She was breathing hard, her body limp and fulfilled, but she managed to open her brilliant green eyes and smile. He threaded her fingers with his and brought them to his lips.

"I want more of you."

She smiled her understanding and nodded with no thought of denying him. Lifting her head off the bed she found his mouth and kissed him, this time letting her tongue explore the depths of him. Her touch set off a ticking bomb in his chest, his gut and his mind. He broke away from her lips, letting his tongue discover her ear, neck and shoulder before coming to her breasts. His hand kneaded one while he suckled the other almost frantically. The dark, rosy-pink tips were swollen and rigid and he suckled first one then the other. Tallie moaned and arched her back, offering herself to him.

When she raised her legs and arched her hips toward his, Cole knew he wasn't going to hold out much longer. With his fingers threaded through her silky black hair and his lips on hers, he began to move.

He pushed in farther, time after time. Her incredible silkiness was so amazing. He inhaled the rich scent of her body; she smelled like lavender, with a hint of wild Texas sage. She altered her position and he knew. He knew what she needed, what she wanted. He felt her still then cry out as the whirlwind carried them both to the heavens and kept them there.

Finally, breathing hard, he fell to one side of her, pulling the edge of the comforter around her. She moved enough to place her head on his shoulder and, with his arms holding her close, he fell into the sweet oblivion he hadn't known in forever, going to a place it seemed only Tallie could take him.

The next morning, Cole slowly came awake with the memories of the night before vivid in his mind. Tallie was still asleep, her head still nestled on his shoulder. Her long hair fanned her shoulders and spread over his chest. She was as beautiful and incredible as ever. She had such passion. Such a wildness that carried him into the realms of the untamed. Their actions were driven by something stronger than passion. It was fierce and uncontrollable, sex in its rawest form. He felt his body getting hard at the thought. He would stay in this bed with her all day and into the night if he could talk her into it. He had never once thought of staying with a woman so long, needing her to stay with no end in sight as they made love over and over again.

Regretfully, business awaited, both hers and his. He pushed the covers back and got out of bed. With one last look at the woman still asleep on the bed, he turned and walked to his room.

Tallie woke in an empty bed. She knew Cole had held her through the night. It was the best sleep she'd had in a long time. Maybe since New Orleans. She smiled at the thought. The sun was just cresting over the horizon when she made her way into the bathroom. She hadn't expected last night to happen but she wasn't sorry. In fact, she felt just the opposite. Cole was an incredible lover. Smiling, she padded to the shower. The water was warm, streaming over her head and down her back as she grabbed for the exotic-smelling soap.

She had just stepped out of the shower and finished dressing when the nausea hit. She couldn't do much more of this, she thought to herself. It had to stop soon. Trembling, she reached out for a towel and wiped her mouth. Standing, she turned toward the sink for the toothbrush and ran straight into Cole.

He was frowning, a look of concern covering his features.

"Do I need to call the doctor?" he asked.

She shook her head. "No, it's just…"

"Tallie, don't tell me it's just a bug. No one gets a virus that lasts this long. Whatever it is, you can tell me."

She had to tell him. To continue to withhold the news was deceitful and just wrong. And if she kept the secret too long, he might think she was trying to set him up. If he hated her for it, so be it. She turned to face him.

"Cole, I was afraid to tell you, but I can't go on living a lie. What I have is morning sickness. I'm pregnant."

The silence in the room was deafening. Cole stared at her as if trying to find some sign she was joking. She saw his Adam's apple bob in his throat as he swallowed hard.

His eyes narrowed while his jaw worked overtime. "You're saying you're pregnant and I'm the father?"

"Yes. It…it happened in New Orleans."

She watched as he swallowed, his features turning dark. He turned away, as though he couldn't look at her anymore.

"That's impossible."

"I assure you it isn't."

Silence cut through the room like a knife. He rested his hands on his hips.

"That was almost five months ago. And you are just telling me now?"

"Until two months ago, I didn't know who you were. Then I didn't know how to tell you."

"What do you want, Tallie?"

Her quick intake of breath filled the silence. "I don't want anything."

Her heart beat wildly in her chest while alarms rang in her ears. This was it. What would he do?

"When were you going to tell me?"

"I don't know."

"What does that mean exactly?" The pure anger in his voice made her jump.

"It means that as soon as I told you, I knew you would accuse me of...all sorts of terrible things. Getting pregnant on purpose at the very least. Of being a gold digger. A tramp." She looked away. "I couldn't deal with that."

"Did you, Tallie? Did you become pregnant on purpose?"

She could only look at him as her eyes filled with tears. "No." It was a whisper, but the best she could do as one tear slid down her face. That Cole had even asked the question was almost more than she could take. "No. I'd just earned my Ph.D. and was about to start on a career that had been a lifelong dream. The last thing I ever expected was to get pregnant."

He looked down at the floor as though the answer was there. "It won't work, you know. Regardless of the planning, the backing, whatever determination you have, it will not work. You're not the first and you probably won't be the last to try this."

Tallie couldn't pretend she didn't know what he was saying. He thought she was using her pregnancy to scam money out of him. She didn't know what to do now. She'd played this scene out in her mind a hundred times but it always stopped with him calling her on it. She'd never ventured to imagine what would happen next.

"What did you hope to achieve by coming here?" He turned and looked at her again and she fought not to cringe at the rage in his eyes. "Does this…dig, this search for a lost civilization, have any basis in fact?"

"What does it matter? You won't believe anything I say."

She reached out to open the door and saw that her hands were shaking. Not surprising. In less than fifteen minutes Cole had gone from the sexy man she was falling in love with to the deadly, dangerous man she'd encountered when she first showed up on his land. A man that any sane person would stay well away from.

"If it's proven to be my child, I will take care of it, certainly. And likewise the mother of the child."

"I'm not asking for anything from you." She opened the door as the first tear fell from her eyes.

"I don't want anything. I can take care of myself. I just wanted you to know that you're going to be a father."

With that said, she marched down the hall, her heart broken into small pieces. Her mind was a jumble of twisted thoughts. She had to get her clothes… had to pack up her things… Cole hated her for something she hadn't intentionally done…she had to talk to the girls…

"I'm flying out this afternoon on business." His voice carried down the hall. "Pick out a dress and some wedding rings if you wish. When I return in five days, we will be married."

That brought her to an immediate stop. Slowly she turned to face him, to face his anger.

"I'm not marrying anyone."

"You will be here when I return and we will be married. In fact, there's no time like the present to get the license."

"No." She spun on her heel and continued toward the back door.

Heavy hands gripped her shoulders and she was turned around. "Do not push me, Tallie."

"Why? What will you do? Threaten to destroy the dig? Sue the museum? You know, I feel sorry for you. The very first time I saw you it saddened me that you were so alone. But now, I realize that's the way you want it. You are going to end up a lonely old man who will look back on your life with regrets. But I won't be there to see it."

"I wish I could believe you because I almost

bought the whole package. Wife, children, family, a permanent home. You, of all people, didn't have to do a goddamned thing. I was falling for you. I thought…"

"What? What did you think, Cole?" The tears she'd fought so hard to hide rolled down her face. Her heart felt as though it was breaking in two.

"I thought you were the first honest person I'd ever met."

She couldn't stop the small cry that left her throat. Her heart shattered. Into millions of tiny pieces. She had never felt such pain. She lost the battle to control herself as the tears ran in waves down her cheeks. She wanted to scream at him, *I'm not lying to you!*

"I'm a realist, Cole. You are not the average person. I imagine that you and your advisors have to contend with schemers trying to get some of your money every day. I'm not one of them. But I have no way to prove it. I didn't tell you because I didn't want to see that look of betrayal in your eyes."

"There is no look of betrayal. We will marry as soon as I can arrange it."

"No, we won't. I refuse to marry a man who doesn't love me. And you just made it clear that you don't believe me or want anything more to do with me. That isn't love."

"I'm just curious, Tallie. Was the entire New Orleans thing staged?"

"*What?*"

"Was it all part of some plan?"

"There was no plan." Her voice was dull, as though the soul inside her body had given up.

He let out a sigh. "I would think by now you would be willing to come clean. But, no matter—we *are* getting married. No way is my son or daughter going to be born without my name whether the baby was conceived under false pretenses or not. It isn't how I roll. It isn't how this family operates."

"I'm not marrying anyone. I've been through a painful breakup once. I'm not about to go through that again by entering into a marriage I know won't last." She looked at Cole. "Based on what you just said, you must have doubts that you're the father."

He thought about that question. "Should I?"

"No. I'll do the test. That's only fair. But I don't want to marry you, Cole."

"That, my dear, is too damn bad."

Tallie tried to work but her heart wasn't in it. The girls seemed to know something was wrong but didn't approach her and she was grateful. Cole had left after he'd taken her to the doctor's office for blood work then to city hall to apply for a marriage license.

He had looked at her then, his usually golden eyes a flat brown, his mouth pulled into a straight line, his dark brows drawn into a frown. "I expect you to be here when I return."

His words were daggers straight to her heart. He had dropped her off at the mansion, picked up his briefcase and, without another word, walked out the door. She'd fallen onto the leather sofa and hadn't stopped crying for hours. Or was it days? And she had not heard from him since that moment.

She stayed for only one reason: she loved him. She could put herself in his place and doing so helped her understand the pain she'd brought to his doorstep. She felt duty-bound to try to do as he asked when all she really wanted was to run away and hide.

At 4:00 p.m. she called a halt to the day. Rain clouds were hovering and the temperature dropped into the low eighties. She stepped back and looked around her. The only place to go was up. Into the cliffs. There might be caves she hadn't spotted yet. Five months into her pregnancy, she debated if she could climb a ladder. Probably not the smartest thing to do.

After herding the girls to the RV and saying good evening to the two cowboys who arrived for their evening watch, she ambled to her old car and headed for the ranch. She could think of a thousand places she'd rather be.

And the next five days went pretty much the same way. She went to the dig site, worked with the girls until four in the afternoon, then returned to the mansion for another lonely night. She still hadn't heard from Cole since their argument. He hadn't called. It should have made her happy but instead she felt dead inside. This situation was not going to work out well.

But tonight, on entering the house, she immediately heard his voice. He must be in his office talking on the phone.

"Chances are meant to be taken, Matt," she heard Cole say. "In business. Not on a personal basis."

There was a silence while Cole listened to the person on the other end of the line.

"No, I really didn't give it a second thought, which was stupid on my part. She was hot and willing and I saw no reason to abstain. She had good references, the family liked her... A few months later she tells me she's pregnant. I used protection. In this day and time I'd be a fool not to. It was then I began to question her and everything about her. I hope like hell you did the same in your situation."

There was another silence. Was Cole talking about their time in New Orleans? She had always prided herself that she wasn't an eavesdropper but it would take a bomb to pry her away from that door.

"What are you going to do?"

Silence.

"Think about this, Matt. She's probably after money. It never fails. And usually there is another man touted as just a friend that's the real father of the baby. He is also the banker. And unless you catch him, he will clean you out. Right now she could take you for everything you're worth. Beat her to the punch and offer her a payoff up front. Let her know your suspicions. If she even considers it, you will have your answer."

Another silence.

"Then all I can tell you is to have your attorneys draw up an ironclad prenup. I'm afraid you're gonna need it. I hope I'm wrong but I haven't seen a woman yet that didn't have those twenty-four-carat stars in her eyes. They will even track you down to get some of it."

Long silence.

"Well, good luck. Keep me posted."

Tallie tried to swallow but her throat had gone dry. Quickly she hurried away from the door, down the hall and out to her car. She felt shocked but her mind told her she shouldn't have been surprised. What else had she expected?

Tallie wanted to ask him how much longer this would go on. How much punishment did he intend to dish out for something that was equally his fault? But she didn't. The overheard phone call had pretty much said it all. She needed to leave. Immediately. Before he tried to force her into a marriage that was wrong on so many levels.

Everything bad she'd imagined happening if Cole found out about the pregnancy was coming true. His words had penetrated her shield of self-protection like a laser cutting through butter. What he'd said hurt deeply. He'd spoken of her like some vicious, impersonal stranger. He considered her someone who expected money for a romp in the bedroom. Now he felt compelled to marry her and give their baby a name. He had described their relationship in such a cold, unfeeling way.

She had never had sex without caring for the person she was with, but realistically that's exactly what she'd done. Knowing how he felt about her brought back the tears. And she couldn't blame Cole. She couldn't blame anyone but herself.

She didn't have to be told twice that she wasn't wanted. She would leave with all possible speed. Returning to the dig wouldn't accomplish anything. He would find her there—if he even bothered to look. She would leave her things and arrange for someone to pick them up later.

She climbed inside her old Ford and started the engine. It was past time to go home.

Cole emerged from his office sometime later, tired but stimulated by the conversation he'd just had with the CEO of a company they'd been trying to do a deal with for about four years. The man had finally looked at the figures and was suddenly interested in a merger and the potential money he would make.

Cole smelled food cooking in the kitchen and headed in that direction. Andre was busy making supper.

"I will have this ready for you in about ten minutes, Mr. Cole."

"That will be fine, Andre. Have you seen Dr. Finley?"

The chef looked at him with a confused expression. "Dr. Finley left. She called Carson and said she would send for her things."

Left? Tallie was gone? "What time did she leave?"

"I'm not sure. A couple of hours ago at least. Carson would know."

"Did she say where she was going?"

"No, sir. She did seem quite distressed but all she said to me was goodbye."

Cole thanked Andre and walked into the den. Tallie had actually left. That was a first. Usually it took a herculean effort to get a woman to leave once she showed her hand. Did Tallie expect him to follow her? To track her down and demand she come back? She was in for a surprise if she did.

He hated being played. He was tired of it happening over and over again. Women saw the name Masters and that's all they needed to know. He had actually thought Tallie would still be here now that she had Cole where she wanted him. In fact, that she'd left was a bit unexpected.

Curious, he sped up the stairs and entered the room she'd been using. Her clothes, everything, was there, including the set of wedding rings in the small black case on the dresser. He opened the box. The rings were there, sparkling against the black velvet. So she hadn't taken the rings. It didn't appear she'd taken much of anything. That surprised him.

Returning to the ground level he called out to Martha, "I have to make a quick run to the bank. Hold supper if you can."

When he stepped outside the sky was already turning black. Storm clouds hung low. He saw lightning in the distance; he heard the rumble of thunder. He jumped into the truck and headed toward downtown Calico Springs. It wouldn't take long to sign the papers he needed to sign down at the bank then he could return home and have a nice quiet evening. As he backed out of the parking area, raindrops began to beat against his windshield.

When he rounded the sharp turn just before the town came into view below, he saw the red, blue and yellow lights up ahead. Police had the area roped off, the road closed to one lane while the firemen pulled ropes and ladders from the truck. It was almost the same place where Gina had plunged off the cliff. Without conscious thought, his gaze honed in on the ambulance. By the time he reached the area, his hands were wet, his mouth dry and his heart was beating out of his chest. He slowed and came to a stop. One of the policemen approached the car.

"Sir, you need to keep moving… Oh. Mr. Masters. I didn't realize it was you."

"I had a friend traveling in this area. She would have passed through here. Could you just tell me if that's a Ford wagon at the bottom of the ravine?"

"No, sir. It's an old Chevrolet. Driver is a man, covered in tattoos. It appears he had one too many, was driving too fast and couldn't make the curve. Looks like he will live, though."

Cole let out the breath he'd been holding. "That's very good to know. I appreciate it, officer." When he saw the officer nod his head, Cole continued on. He drove a short distance down the road and pulled over. He drew a deep, shaky breath, striving for calm.

When he had first seen those flashing lights and realized another accident had happened at that turn in the road, he'd almost lost it. Fate couldn't be that cruel. It easily could have been Tallie at the bottom of the cliff. *Oh, God.* Realization came down on his head and shoulders. What had he done?

Tallie was not like Gina and if she had gone over the edge it would be his fault entirely. Torn between relief and worry, he was glad Tallie had not followed the same path as Gina but he was still concerned. Where was she? He once again turned the truck around and headed home. His business at the bank could wait.

Now that the news of the pending birth had soaked in, he was excited about their child.

Tallie was pregnant. She'd said that he was the father and he should have believed her. It was the same scene as had played out with Gina, only that child had not been his. But Cole knew in his gut that Tallie wouldn't lie to him. He'd screwed up big time.

He'd handled the knowledge she was pregnant badly. He'd done exactly what she'd thought he would do: accuse her of trying to pull a fast one. Of getting pregnant on purpose. He still felt his heart sink to his knees every time he thought about what he'd said. He may have lost Tallie and his son or daughter permanently after his cruel allegations.

She had tied one on at a bar in New Orleans and taken a chance on giving herself to a stranger. It must have taken everything she'd had even with the help of alcohol, to give herself to him. But she'd picked the wrong man. He had been so intent on seeing every woman as a lying, conniving cheat that he hadn't considered staying with her long enough to talk the next morning. He'd walked out on her. What a fool he'd been.

Damn. This was all his fault. He'd screwed up royally. First he'd gotten her pregnant then blamed her that it happened. He had to find her. He had to apologize, to explain. Hell, he had to ask for her forgiveness. He'd never done that before, but he imagined groveling would be involved. A tinge of pure fear ran through his body that even if he found her, she would reject him. It's what he deserved. But he loved her and that was a first for Cole. He would be proud of their child. Proud to call Tallie his wife. He was willing to do whatever it took.

He tried calling her repeatedly but there was no answer. He didn't have her boss's home number. He would have to wait until tomorrow to contact Dr. Sterling. Then he would make her listen. How could he have insinuated she had lied about the baby and accuse her of getting pregnant on purpose? He knew better. Tallie was not Gina. And he had pushed Tallie too far. He just hoped to God she would listen to him. When he found her. *If* he found her.

The morning came. Then another and another. No Tallie. Her boss at the museum refused to give him her address, citing the laws he would be breaking if he did. He'd dismissed the college students helping her on the site with instructions to call him if they had news of Tallie, but he hadn't heard anything from them. And Tallie was still not answering the only number he had for her.

Tallie was gone. She was smart enough that if she didn't want to be found, he wouldn't find her. He felt as though part of him had been ripped out and thrown away.

He ran a hand over his face. He had to find her. *But why?* asked a little voice in his head. *Isn't this what you wanted?*

Cole sat on the large sofa in the den, the last moments they'd had together running through his mind. Tallie was so amazing, so different than Gina, they could be two separate species. Tallie's intelligence was off the charts. Her sense of humor had him laughing when at times he wanted to break down and have a fit of frustration. Her natural beauty was unsurpassed.

He needed to find her. He needed to sit down and listen this time to what she had to say and to keep his temper under control. He grabbed his cell and called the little motel in Calico Springs. She wasn't a registered guest.

If Tallie had intentionally disappeared, neither he nor his security staff would find her. Her family would stick together and protect one of their own. And what in the hell was he going to do?

Fourteen

Three months later

Cole had come home to pick up some papers and was on his way back out when the phone rang. "Yeah?" he answered coldly.

"Is this Mr. Masters?" a woman asked.

"Yes, it is. Who is this?"

"You probably won't remember me. My name is Kathy Brown and I was one of the four students who worked for Dr. Finley. You gave all of us your cell number in case of any emergency."

"I remember you, Kathy. Have you heard from Dr. Finley? Is she okay?"

"My mother is a nurse at Medical Central Hospital in Dallas. She knew I was working for Dr. Finley and mentioned that she was admitted as a patient."

"She's in the hospital?" His heart sank to his knees. Had something happened to her? All the worst scenarios raced across his mind. Cole was holding back a scream, a demand to know where she was, but he didn't want to frighten the young student.

"Yes, sir," she replied. "She's been there for a week. It's something about her pregnancy. Something has gone wrong." She paused as if putting thought to what else to say. "I just didn't know if you knew. Dr. Finley is such a nice lady and I know you were friends."

Assuring Kathy that Tallie would be all right, as though he actually knew something she didn't—he thanked her for calling and hung up.

Cole's heart began to slam against the wall of his chest. He immediately called for a driver. No time for a shower. Since Tallie had left, Cole had spent his days in the main barn, mucking stalls, grooming, exercising colts in training, his work forgotten until he could find Tallie. Now, he wanted to be there with her as fast as possible.

The helicopter ride to Dallas was excruciatingly long. And when they got there and switched to a limo to drive into the city, every red light seemed to take an hour to pass. Finally the tall, fourteen-story hospital loomed ahead. His driver pulled up under the pergola and Cole bailed. By the time he stood in front of the double doors leading to the ICU he felt as though he'd just run a marathon. With every step he worried. *Does she want me here? Will she see me?* The shoulda's and coulda's followed him the whole way.

He went to the nurses' station in the ICU and asked where Tallie's room was. The attendant looked something up on the computer and said, "Ms. Finley has been taken to surgery. Up two floors. There is a waiting room."

Cole ran for the elevator. When he got off, he quickly followed the signs to the surgical unit. Eventually a nurse answered the doorbell leading to the surgical ward.

"I'm looking for Tallie Finley."

"And you are?"

"Her husband, Cole Finley." He hardly gave the lie a second thought.

"She has just been taken to recovery. I'll let them know you're here. Have a seat in the waiting room across the hall. We'll notify you when you can see her."

Recovery. That was good—wasn't it? It had been twelve weeks since Tallie had left the ranch. A quick calculation put her at about eight and a half months pregnant.

The minutes slowly ticked by. Every time he looked at his watch, only three or four minutes had passed. He stood and walked to the window. People were coming and going, some smiling, some weeping. He gripped his hands into tight fists. Tallie had to be okay. She just had to be.

Finally a nurse came into the room calling out for

Mr. Finley. Cole followed her into Recovery. Tallie was asleep; her face looked ashen. He couldn't not touch her. He went to the bed and picked up one small, soft hand. She stirred and blinked her eyes as though she couldn't believe he was there, standing next to her. Whether that was good or bad remained to be seen.

"You're here," she whispered as if it was a struggle to speak. Her eyes fell away and closed as she concentrated on something going on with her body. She suddenly gripped his hand. Hard. "Are they all right? The babies?"

The babies? Was she delusional? "Sure, honey," he said to comfort her. "They are going to be fine."

Cole wanted to ask why she hadn't called him. He wanted to ask why she hadn't wanted him to know she was here. And why had she referred to his son or daughter as the *babies*? A thousand questions swirled in his mind but, at the moment, none of them mattered. And he had to ask her forgiveness.

A nurse bustled in and proceeded to check Tallie's vitals. She looked at Cole. "Are you the proud father?"

"Yes," he said firmly, his gaze going to Tallie. "I am indeed."

Tears filled Tallie's eyes. A silent message passed between her and Cole. One of pride and acceptance.

"You guys have two beautiful baby boys. We think they are both gonna be just fine. May have to stay in the incubator a couple of weeks, but they are breathing on their own and screaming for that bottle. Give it a while for the drugs to wear off and we can get you into a private room. Then you can feed them if you wish, Mrs. Finley."

"Oh, yes," Tallie answered.

"Your vitals look good. Give it about an hour and someone will come and get you," the nurse concluded and bustled out the door.

Cole could only stare. Twins. He needed to sit down.

"Cole, are you all right?"

He silently shook his head. "Hon, we are having twins. Twins."

He heard her chuckle. "We *have* twins, you nut cake. Why are you here?"

"I love you, Tallie." He kissed the palm of her hand.

"But you don't believe there is such a thing as love."

"I was wrong. I was stupid. I can't call what I feel anything else. I've honestly never felt this way before about anyone. When I thought you had died… Tallie, can you forgive me for reacting the way I did? Forgive me for doubting? And marry me, Tallie. My life won't be complete without you in it. I know we can make it work."

"You're not ready to settle down with a wife and children. You have your work. I'm not going to be the one to negatively impact your life."

"You are the first and only woman I've ever been this drawn to. And you will be the last. I don't want anyone but you." He wanted to scream it to the whole world but gritted his teeth to maintain control. "Marry me, Tallie. Marry me because you love me and because you believe I love you. Marry me with no regrets."

"I love you, Cole. And if you're sure, yes."

"Yes? You will marry me?"

"I'm an easy sell when it comes to you." She smiled and the twinkle was back in those emerald green eyes.

He bent over the bed and touched his lips to hers. It felt so right. He placed a hand on her head and followed with more kisses, loving this woman with everything he had inside. "You are so beautiful," he told her and knew she could see the honesty in his face.

A little while later, a team of nurses came into the recovery room, and rolled Tallie's bed down the hall to a private room.

"Mr....Finley?" one of the nurses said to him. "While we get her settled in, if you would like to feed the babies with your wife, stop by the nursing station. They will provide a mask and gown."

Feeling excited and numb at the same time, Cole did as the woman suggested. When Tallie was settled in her new room, two nurses placed one newborn infant wrapped in a little blue blanket in his arms and gave one to Tallie.

Cole could only stare at the tiny new life he held. He was perfect. His cry sounded more like a kitten's than a baby's but it was the most beautiful sound Cole had ever heard. He caught Tallie's attention and mouthed "I love you." She smiled and said it right back. There was no expressing the love that grew in his chest at seeing his soon-to-be wife feed one newborn son then the other. Two sons. She had given him two incredible miracles.

The babies fed and back in the nursery, Cole left Tallie alone to rest. He'd kissed her goodbye with a promise that he would be back.

Had she agreed to marry Cole Masters? Still full of emotion, she felt tears of happiness welling up in her eyes. For the first time in her life, she was loved, truly loved, by an incredible man. She never thought she would trust another, yet there was no doubt in her mind that Cole loved her. With that in mind, she closed her eyes.

An hour later she awoke to a soft knock. "Come in."

It was Cole. He was grinning ear to ear while he held the largest bouquet of red roses she'd ever seen. Setting them on a table, he moved to Tallie and gave her a deep, meaningful kiss. "How are you feeling?"

"Pretty good, considering." She pushed herself up against the pillows. It was time to ask him a difficult question that had been bothering her.

"Cole, the day I left the ranch I overheard you on the phone talking to someone named Matt. You spelled it out pretty clearly that I had gotten pregnant on purpose and only wanted your money." Tears filled her eyes and she snatched a tissue from the bedside table. "If you feel that way, why did you come here? Why would you want to marry me?"

Cole sat on the edge of the bed and took the tissue from her, gently wiping her eyes. "I wasn't talking about you, sweetheart. I was talking about Gina, my ex-wife. She and her boyfriend set up this elaborate plan to get me to marry her so she could extract money, tens of millions of dollars, from a few of my bank accounts. The night I kicked her out, she drove too fast around a curve on the edge of a cliff and lost control of the car. She died immediately. So did the baby she was carrying. I never found out if it was mine or the other guy's."

"Oh, Cole, I'm so sorry."

"It made me bitter and hard and unforgiving. When I lashed out at you it was really Gina in my mind's eye. I will regret that until the day I die."

Tallie raised their joined hands to her face and kissed his palm. "I'm sorry you had to go through that."

"God, I love you, Tallie. I actually thought I was in love with her. You showed me what real love is."

Suddenly there was a knock on the door and an entourage of people walked into the room. She recognized Wade Masters, Cole's older brother. And next to Cole were Chance and his wife Holly. Before she could say hello to anyone, another man stepped forward.

"Hello, Dr. Finley," he said. "Congratulations. You and Cole have two beautiful sons."

"Thank you." What was Reverend Blackhawk

from her hometown doing here? And what was the formal-looking paper he held in his hand?

"You said you would marry me," Cole told her softly. "I intend to hold you to your word."

"Are you sure?" she asked him. "Now? Here?"

Cole leaned over her and whispered in her ear. "Yes. And when you heal, I intend to show you exactly how sure I am."

Tallie signed her name and handed the form to the reverend, who passed it on to Wade, Holly and Chance to sign as official witnesses. Some twenty minutes later, after Holly did her hair and added some lipstick and a hint of blush, they said their vows and Tallie became Mrs. Cole Masters. His lips had never felt better on hers. When the clapping began, Cole lifted his head and winked at her.

It was, indeed, a beautiful day.

Epilogue

All the people at the museum were gathered around, wanting to have the opportunity to get closer to Tallie's babies.

Tallie left the dual stroller just outside her office as her friends oohed and aahed. Stepping into her office she proceeded to power up her computer. She needed to check the dates of certain meetings and what digs were scheduled for the next month. She glanced at her watch and wondered where Cole was. He'd said he would meet her here.

Outside, she heard the small crowd of people greeting Cole, who had apparently just arrived. Pulling up her email software, she began to scan the nearly three months of messages. It was going to take a lot longer to catch up than she'd thought.

"Hi, sweetheart." Cole walked around her desk and planted a deep kiss on her lips. "Happy six-week anniversary." He grinned that adorable grin. Tallie saw the sparks in his eyes and knew today marked the end of the safe period. Romantic evenings and spontaneous sex were back on. They had come close a number of times but Cole had held firm, a trait she'd told him she didn't especially hold in high regard.

"I have a wedding present for you."

She laughed. "Husbands don't give wedding presents. But what do you have?"

A huge smile covered his face as he held up an item about the size of a football. It was wrapped in a blanket and she watched as Cole began to carefully remove it. Gasps from all the people who were crowded in the doorway made her realize they were not alone.

"Presenting one certified pot—well, most of a pot, from your dig. Dr. Sterling has put his stamp of approval on it. It's what you were looking for, Tallie."

"But how…?"

Cole held it out for her to take. "You had been edging ever closer to the cliffs. I took a couple of men and we climbed up the face of the cliff and found the cave you suspected was there. Inside, it's full of pottery, spear-type weapons, jewelry… a whole bunch of things. We didn't enter the cave more than a couple of feet. I wasn't about to incur your wrath by stepping on something priceless. So, the rest is there for you to discover. Now you have proof positive of the origins of your family's people, Tallie. Your grandmother was right."

Woots and laughter filled the air until Dr. Sterling shooed everyone out saying they were going to frighten the babies. Her colleagues took the piece of pottery with them, continuing to gush as it was carefully passed around.

"Cole, if that is, in fact, proof of my people's origins, it might cause problems with building your retreat."

"So, what are you saying? Find another place for my project—which I am willing to do. Or cover the cave back up and forget what's there?" he asked, sitting on the edge of her desk. "That's not happening. I spoke with Dr. Sterling about the possibility of incorporating your discovery in what I'm building. What better way to showcase our American beginnings than including a museum presenting remnants and information from the earliest people who ever lived on the land?"

"You would do that, Cole?"

"You were right, sweetheart. This is so much more important than my project."

Tallie was out of her chair and hugging her husband with the speed of a lightning flash. "Thank you. Thank you, Cole."

"I'll tell you what. You finish up here and let's get you and our two spoiled brats home. I think I know of a way you can thank me."

"Well, what do you know? It just so happens I'm

finished." Tallie reached over and closed the lid of her laptop. "What are we waiting for?"

"Not a single thing."

Cole grabbed the handle of the stroller and escorted Tallie to the big doors of the museum, waving goodbye to all of Tallie's associates. Then he draped his arm around her shoulders and pushed his sons' stroller with the other hand as they headed to the car.

Tallie thought of her grandmother, who had set this all in motion. As her *ipokini* had told her, all things happen for a reason. Tallie believed her. One small map had changed her path forever. Had changed her life and brought her the man of her dreams.

Life just didn't get any better than this.

* * * * *

Pick up these other sexy Western romances from
Golden Heart Award-winning author Lauren Canan!

TERMS OF A TEXAS MARRIAGE
LONE STAR BABY BOMBSHELL
REDEEMING THE BILLIONAIRE SEAL

Available now from Harlequin Desire!

* * *

If you're on Twitter, tell us what you think of
Harlequin Desire! #harlequindesire

*If you like sexy and steamy stories with
strong heroines and irresistible heroes,
you'll love FORGED IN DESIRE by
New York Times bestselling author
Brenda Jackson—featuring Margo Connelly
and Lamar "Striker" Jennings,
the reformed bad boy who'll do anything
to protect her, even if it means lowering
the defenses around his own heart...*

*Turn the page for a sneak peek at
FORGED IN DESIRE!*

PROLOGUE

"FINALLY, WE GET to go home."

Margo Connelly was certain the man's words echoed the sentiment they all felt. The last thing she'd expected when reporting for jury duty was to be sequestered during the entire trial…especially with twelve strangers, more than a few of whom had taken the art of bitching to a whole new level.

She was convinced this had been the longest, if not the most miserable, six weeks of her life, as well as a lousy way to start off the new year. They hadn't been allowed to have any inbound or outbound calls, read the newspapers, check any emails, watch television or listen to the radio. The only good thing was, with the vote just taken, a unanimous decision had been reached and justice would be served. The federal case against Murphy Erickson would finally be over and they would be allowed to go home.

"It's time to let the bailiff know we've reached a decision," Nancy Snyder spoke up, interrupting Margo's thoughts. "I have a man waiting at home, who I haven't seen in six weeks, and I can't wait to get to him."

Lucky you, Margo thought, leaning back in her

chair. She and Scott Dylan had split over a year ago, and the parting hadn't been pretty.

Fortunately, as a wedding-dress designer, she could work from anywhere and had decided to move back home to Charlottesville. She could be near her uncle Frazier, her father's brother and the man who'd become her guardian when her parents had died in a house fire when she was ten. He was her only living relative and, although they often butted heads, she had missed him while living in New York.

A knock on the door got everyone's attention. The bailiff had arrived. Hopefully, in a few hours it would all be over and the judge would release them. She couldn't wait to get back to running her business. Six weeks had been a long time away. Lucky for her she had finished her last order in time for the bride's Christmas wedding. But she couldn't help wondering how many new orders she might have missed while on jury duty.

The bailiff entered and said, "The judge has called the court back in session for the reading of the verdict. We're ready to escort you there."

Like everyone else in the room, Margo stood. She was ready for the verdict to be read. It was only after this that she could get her life back.

"FOREMAN, HAS THE JURY reached a verdict?" the judge asked.

"Yes, we have, Your Honor."

The courtroom was quiet as the verdict was read.

"We, the jury, find Murphy Erickson guilty of murder."

Suddenly Erickson bowled over and laughed. It made the hairs on the necks of everyone in attendance stand up. The outburst prompted the judge to hit his gavel several times. "Order in the courtroom. Counselor, quiet the defendant or he will be found in contempt of court."

"I don't give a damn about any contempt," Erickson snarled loudly. "You!" he said, pointing a finger at the judge. "Along with everyone else in this courtroom, you have just signed your own death warrant. As long as I remain locked up, someone in here will die every seventy-two hours." His gaze didn't miss a single individual.

Pandemonium broke out. The judge pounded his gavel, trying to restore order. Police officers rushed forward to subdue Erickson and haul him away. But the sound of his threats echoed loudly in Margo's ears.

CHAPTER ONE

LAMAR "STRIKER" JENNINGS walked into the hospital room, stopped and then frowned. "What the hell is he doing working from bed?"

"I asked myself the same thing when I got his call for us to come here," Striker's friend Quasar Patterson said, sitting lazily in a chair with his long legs stretched out in front of him.

"And you might as well take a seat like he told us to do," another friend, Stonewall Courson, suggested, while pointing to an empty chair. "Evidently it will take more than a bullet to slow down Roland."

Roland Summers, CEO of Summers Security Firm, lay in the hospital bed, staring at them. Had it been just last week that the man had been fighting for his life after foiling an attempted carjacking?

"You still look like shit, Roland. Shouldn't you be trying to get some rest instead of calling a meeting?" Striker asked, sliding his tall frame into the chair. He didn't like seeing Roland this way. They'd been friends a long time, and he couldn't ever recall the man being sick. Not even with a cold. Well, at least he was alive. That damn bullet could have taken him out and Striker didn't want to think about that.

"You guys have been keeping up with the news?" Roland asked in a strained voice, interrupting Striker's thoughts.

"We're aware of what's going on, if that's what you want to know," Stonewall answered. "Nobody took Murphy Erickson's threat seriously."

Roland made an attempt to nod his head. "And now?"

"And now people are panicking. Phones at the office have been ringing off the hook. I'm sure every protective security service in town is booked solid. Everyone in the courtroom that day is either in hiding or seeking protection, and with good reason," Quasar piped in to say. "The judge, clerk reporter and bailiff are all dead. All three were gunned down within seventy-two hours of each other."

"The FBI is working closely with local law enforcement, and they figure it's the work of the same assassin," Striker added. "I heard they anticipate he'll go after someone on the jury next."

"Which is why I called the three of you here. There was a woman on the jury who I want protected. It's personal."

"Personal?" Striker asked, lifting a brow. He knew Roland dated off and on, but he'd never been serious with anyone. He was always quick to say that his wife, Becca, had been his one and only love.

"Yes, personal. She's a family member."

The room got quiet. That statement was even more baffling since, as far as the three of them knew, Roland didn't have any family…at least not anymore.

They were all aware of his history. He'd been a cop, who'd discovered some of his fellow officers on the take. Before he could blow the whistle he'd been framed and sent to prison for fifteen years. Becca had refused to accept his fate and worked hard to get him a new trial. He served three years before finally leaving prison but not before the dirty cops murdered Roland's wife. All the cops involved had eventually been brought to justice and charged with the death of Becca Summers, in addition to other crimes.

"You said she's family?" Striker asked, looking confused.

"Yes, although I say that loosely since we've never officially met. I know who she is, but she doesn't know I even exist." Roland then closed his eyes, and Striker knew he had to be in pain.

"Man, you need to rest," Quasar spoke up. "You can cover this with us another time."

Roland's eyes flashed back open. "No, we need to talk now. I need one of you protecting her right away."

Nobody said anything for a minute and then Striker asked, "What relation is she to you, man?"

"My niece. To make a long story short, years ago my mom got involved with a married man. He broke things off when his wife found out about the affair but not before I was conceived. I always knew the identity of my father. I also knew about his other two, older sons, although they didn't know about me. I guess you can say I was the old man's secret.

"One day after I'd left for college, I got a call from

my mother letting me know the old man was dead but he'd left me something in his will."

Striker didn't say anything, thinking that at least Roland's old man had done right by him in the end. To this day, his own poor excuse of a father hadn't even acknowledged his existence. "That's when your two brothers found out about you?" he asked.

"Yes. Their mother found out about me, as well. She turned out to be a real bitch. Even tried blocking what Connelly had left for me in the will. But she couldn't. The old man evidently had anticipated her making such a move and made sure the will was ironclad. He gave me enough to finish college without taking out student loans with a little left over."

"Good for him," Quasar said. "What about your brothers? How did they react to finding out about you?"

"The eldest acted like a dickhead," Roland said without pause. "The other one's reaction was just the opposite. His name was Murdock and he reached out to me afterward. I would hear from him from time to time. He would call to see how I was doing."

Roland didn't say anything for a minute, his face showing he was struggling with strong emotions. "Murdock is the one who gave Becca the money to hire a private investigator to reopen my case. I never got the chance to thank him."

"Why?" Quasar asked.

Roland drew in a deep breath and then said, "Murdock and his wife were killed weeks before my new trial began."

"How did they die?"

"House fire. Fire department claimed faulty wiring. I never believed it but couldn't prove otherwise. Luckily their ten-year-old daughter wasn't home at the time. She'd been attending a sleepover at one of her friends' houses."

"You think those dirty cops took them out, too?" Stonewall asked.

"Yes. While I could link Becca's death to those corrupt cops, there wasn't enough evidence to connect Murdock's and his wife's deaths."

Stonewall nodded. "What happened to the little girl after that?"

"She was raised by the other brother. Since the old lady had died by then, he became her guardian." Roland paused a minute and then added, "He came to see me this morning."

"Who? Your brother? The dickhead?" Quasar asked with a snort.

"Yes," Roland said, and it was obvious he was trying not to grin. "When he walked in here it shocked the hell out of me. Unlike Murdock, he never reached out to me, and I think he even resented Murdock for doing so."

"So what the fuck was his reason for showing up here today?" Stonewall asked. "He'd heard you'd gotten shot and wanted to show some brotherly concern?" It was apparent by Stonewall's tone he didn't believe that was the case.

"Umm, let me guess," Quasar then said languidly. "He had a change of heart, especially now that his niece's life is in danger. Now he wants your help. I assume this is the same niece you want protected."

"Yes, to both. He'd heard I'd gotten shot and claimed he was concerned. Although he's not as much of a dickhead as before, I sensed a little resentment is still there. But not because I'm his father's bastard—a part of me believes he's gotten over that."

"What, then?" Striker asked.

"I think he blames me for Murdock's death. He didn't come out and say that, but he did let me know he was aware of the money Murdock gave Becca to get me a new trial and that he has similar suspicions regarding the cause of their deaths. That's why, when he became his niece's guardian, he sent her out of the country to attend an all-girls school with tight security in London for a few years. He didn't bring her back to the States until after those bad cops were sent to jail."

"So the reason he showed up today was because he thought sending you on a guilt trip would be the only way to get you to protect your niece?" Striker asked angrily. Although Roland had tried hiding it, Striker could clearly see the pain etched in his face whenever he spoke.

"Evidently. I guess it didn't occur to him that making sure she is protected is something I'd want to do. I owe Murdock, although I don't owe Frazier Connelly a damn thing."

"Frazier Connelly?" Quasar said, sitting up straight in his chair. "*The* Frazier Connelly of Connelly Enterprises?"

"One and the same."

Nobody said anything for a while. Then Striker asked, "Your niece—what's her name?"

"Margo. Margo Connelly."

"And she doesn't know anything about you?" Stonewall asked. "Are you still the family's well-kept secret?"

Roland nodded. "Frazier confirmed that today, and I prefer things to stay that way. If I could, I would protect her. I can't, so I need one of you to do it for me. Hopefully, it won't be long before the assassin that Erickson hired is apprehended."

Striker eased out of his chair. Roland, of all people, knew that, in addition to working together, he, Quasar and Stonewall were the best of friends. They looked out for each other and watched each other's back. And if needed they would cover Roland's back, as well. Roland was more than just their employer—he was their close friend, mentor and the voice of reason, even when they really didn't want one. "Stonewall is handling things at the office in your absence, and Quasar is already working a case. That leaves me. Don't worry about a thing, Roland. I've got it covered. Consider it done."

MARGO CONNELLY STARED up at her uncle. "A body-guard? Do you really think that's necessary, Uncle Frazier? I understand extra policemen are patrolling the streets."

"That's not good enough. Why should I trust a bunch of police officers?"

"Why shouldn't you?" she countered, not for the first time wondering what her uncle had against cops.

"I have my reasons, but this isn't about me—this is about you and your safety. I refuse to have you placed in any danger. What's the big deal? You've had a bodyguard before."

Yes, she'd had one before. Right after her parents' deaths, when her uncle had become her guardian. He had shipped her off to London for three years. She'd reckoned he'd been trying to figure out what he, a devout bachelor, was to do with a ten-year-old. When she returned to the United States, Apollo remained her bodyguard. When she turned fourteen, she fought hard for a little personal freedom. But she'd always known the chauffeurs Uncle Frazier hired could do more than drive her to and from school. More than once she'd seen the guns they carried.

"Yes, but that was then and this is now, Uncle Frazier. I can look after myself."

"Haven't you been keeping up with the news?" he snapped. "Three people are dead. All three were in that courtroom with you. Erickson is making sure his threat is carried out."

"And more than likely whoever is committing these murders will be caught before there can be another shooting. I understand the three were killed while they were away from home. I have enough paperwork to catch up on here for a while. I didn't even leave my house today."

"You don't think a paid assassin will find you here? Alone? You either get on board with having a bodyguard or you move back home. It's well secured there."

Margo drew in a deep breath. Back home was the Connelly estate. Yes, it was secure, with its state-of-the-art surveillance system. While growing up, she'd thought of the ten-acre property, surrounded by a tall wrought iron fence and cameras watching her every move, as a prison. Now she couldn't stand the thought of staying there for any long period of time...especially if Liz was still in residence.

Margo's forty-five-year-old uncle had never married and claimed he had his reasons for never wanting to. But that didn't keep him from occasionally having a live-in mistress under his roof. His most recent was Liz Tillman and, as far as Margo was concerned, the woman was a *gold digger*.

"It's final. A bodyguard will be here around the clock to protect you until this madness is over."

Margo didn't say anything. She wondered if at any time it had crossed her uncle's mind that they were at her house, not his, and she was no longer a child but a twenty-six-year-old woman. In a way she knew she should appreciate his concern, but she refused to let anyone order her around.

He was wrong in assuming she hadn't been keeping up with the news. Just because she was trying to maintain a level head didn't mean a part of her wasn't a little worried.

She frowned as she glanced up at him. The last thing she wanted was for him to worry needlessly about her. "I'll give this bodyguard a try...but he better be forewarned not to get underfoot. I have a lot of work to do." She wasn't finished yet. "And another thing, Uncle Frazier," she said, crossing her arms over her chest. "I think you forget sometimes that I'm twenty-six and live on my own. Just because I'm going along with you on this, I hope you don't think you can start bulldozing your way with me."

He glowered at her. "You're stubborn like your father."

She smiled. "I'll take that as a compliment." Dropping her hands, she moved back toward the sofa and sat down, grabbing a magazine off the coffee table to flip through. "So, when do we hire this bodyguard?"

"He's been hired. In fact, I expect him to arrive in a few minutes."

Margo's head jerked up. "What?"

Find out what happens when Margo and Striker come face-to-face in FORGED IN DESIRE by New York Times *bestselling author* *Brenda Jackson.* *Available February 2017 from Brenda Jackson and HQN Books.*

COMING NEXT MONTH FROM

HARLEQUIN®
Desire

Available April 4, 2017

#2509 THE TEN-DAY BABY TAKEOVER
Billionaires and Babies • by Karen Booth
When Sarah Daltry barges into billionaire Aiden Langford's office with his secret baby, he strikes a deal—help him out for ten days as the nanny and he'll help with her new business. Love isn't part of the deal...

#2510 EXPECTING THE BILLIONAIRE'S BABY
Texas Cattleman's Club: Blackmail • by Andrea Laurence
Thirteen years after their breakup, Deacon Chase and Cecelia Morgan meet again...and now he's her billionaire boss! But while Deacon unravels the secrets between them, Cecelia discovers she has a little surprise in store for him, as well...

#2511 PRIDE AND PREGNANCY
by Sarah M. Anderson
Secretly wealthy FBI agent Tom Yellow Bird always puts the job first. But whisking sexy Caroline away to his luxury cabin is above and beyond. And when they end up in bed—and expecting!—it could compromise the most important case of his career...

#2512 HIS EX'S WELL-KEPT SECRET
The Ballantyne Brothers • by Joss Wood
Their weekend in Milan led to a child, but after an accident, rich jeweler Jaeger Ballantyne can't remember any of it! Now Piper Mills is back in his life, asking for his help, and once again he can't resist her...

#2513 THE MAGNATE'S MAIL-ORDER BRIDE
The McNeill Magnates • by Joanne Rock
When a Manhattan billionaire sets his sights on ballerina Sofia Koslov for a marriage of convenience to cover up an expensive family scandal, will she gain the freedom she's always craved, or will it cost her everything?

#2514 A BEAUTY FOR THE BILLIONAIRE
Accidental Heirs • by Elizabeth Bevarly
Hogan has inherited a fortune! He's gone from mechanic to billionaire overnight and can afford to win back the socialite who once broke his heart. So he hires his ex's favorite chef, Chloe, to lure her in, but soon he's falling for the wrong woman...

---

*Desperate to escape her sheltered life, Hayley Thompson
quits her job as church secretary to become personal
assistant to bad-tempered, reclusive, way-too-sexy
Jonathan Bear. But his kiss is more temptation than
she bargained for!*

Read on for a sneak peek at
SEDUCE ME, COWBOY
the latest in Maisey Yates's New York Times *bestselling*
COPPER RIDGE *series!*

This was a mistake. Jonathan Bear was absolutely certain of it. But he had earned millions making mistakes, so what was one more? Nobody else had responded to his ad.

Except for this pale, strange little creature who looked barely twenty and wore the outfit of an eighty-year-old woman.

She was… Well, she wasn't the kind of formidable woman who could stand up to the rigors of working with him.

His sister, Rebecca, would say—with absolutely no tact at all—that he sucked as a boss. And maybe she was right, but he didn't really care. He was busy, and right now he hated most of what he was busy with.

There was irony in that, he knew. He had worked hard all his life. He had built everything he had, brick by brick. And every brick built a stronger wall against all the things he had left behind. Poverty, uncertainty, the lack of respect.

Finally, Jonathan Bear, that poor Indian kid who wasn't worth anything to anyone, bastard son of the biggest bastard in town, had his house on the side of the mountain and more money than he would ever be able to spend.

And he was bored out of his mind.

Boredom, it turned out, worked him into a hell of a temper. He had a feeling Hayley Thompson wasn't strong enough to stand up to that. But he expected to go through a few assistants before he found one who could handle it. She might as well be number one.

"You've got the job," he said. "You can start tomorrow."

Her eyes widened, and he noticed they were a strange shade of blue. Gray in some lights, shot through with a dark, velvet navy that reminded him of the ocean before a storm. It made him wonder if there was some hidden strength there.

They would both find out.

Don't miss
SEDUCE ME, COWBOY
by New York Times *bestselling author Maisey Yates,*
available November 2016 wherever
Harlequin® Desire books and ebooks are sold.

www.Harlequin.com

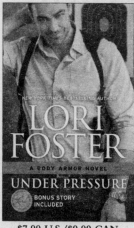